A Lone Star Christmas

A Lone Star Christmas

A Texas Justice Romance

Justine Davis

A Lone Star Christmas

Tule Publishing First Printing, November 2019

The Tule Publishing, Inc.

First Publication by Tule Publishing 2019

Cover design by The Killion Group

ISBN: 978-1-951190-80-4

Dedication

To my beloved and still much missed
mother-in-law,
who was christened
Elia Maria de los Angeles de
Jesus Antoniera de la Cova y Romero
and could have fixed my character name
conundrum in an instant.

Chapter One

DETECTIVE SEAN HIGHWATER sat tapping his finger restlessly on the steering wheel of his unmarked police unit as he watched the people in the park. He'd been restless all day. It must have been Thanksgiving that had thrown him off. It had been so late this year, just two days before the end of the month, that he was still mentally trying to catch up now on the day after. And they were already looking at the Corbyns' tree-trimming open house—the unofficial start of the Christmas season in Last Stand—tomorrow.

He'd never liked the changing date of that holiday anyway. It offended his sense of logic, of rhythm, of pattern and progression. Most other holidays were regular, predictable, never moving from their dates. He had to deal with enough randomness—as in that of the human race—in his work, he didn't like having to deal with it on the calendar, too.

Be thankful They don't screw with everything else the way They did with Washington's birthday. If They'll mess with George Washington just to get a long weekend, They'll do anything.

He wasn't sure who "They" were, just that it was spelled with a capital T.

He was sure that he was among the odd ones. He always had been. Sometimes he wondered what would have become of him if he'd been born to some other family, who maybe weren't as accepting of the quirks of his brain. But he'd been lucky. He'd had his father, a man who loved him whether or not he understood him, until he was eighteen. He'd had Slater, his brilliant brother who truly had understood how his mind worked. He'd had Shane, who had stepped into their father's sizeable boots and held them all together after the grim events that had taken place just down the street from where he sat now, when the Highwater clan had been nearly blasted to pieces forever. And he had his little sister Sage, the girl they had all come together for, and that every one of them would drop everything to help even now.

Then it happened and his finger-tapping stopped. He'd been waiting for this since he'd spotted the knot of kids next to the park's playground. He saw the shift in posture, the arranging of the many against the one.

The taunting had begun.

He'd picked up the vibe the moment he'd seen them, and recognized it instantly. Because many, many times in his life at that age, he'd been on the receiving end. Been the geek, the nerd, the odd one out. The one who liked puzzles and stories more than he liked most people, and video games best of all.

The kid in the blue sweatshirt could be him. The kid he'd been. The sweatshirt had a video game character on it. He didn't know from what game—he'd graduated to first-person shooters at fourteen—but he recognized the style.

And even now, when video games had become mainstream, there were still those who mocked them, and some who did worse than mock the devotees.

Or went after kids who just had that air of being different.

Or just kids smaller than them.

With some bullies, it didn't take much.

And this kid had had the bad luck to run into a handful of them. On a day off from school with time to kill. And now the threats had begun. He knew the cycle well, he'd lived it often enough.

Happy day after Thanksgiving, kid.

He got out of the car. Calculated the distance. Seven seconds, tops. The taunters never saw or heard him coming. He'd gotten very good at silent movement when he'd been that age and been sneaking down to play his games in the dark. Of course, Dad had solved that by confiscating the headphones he wore to keep it silent in the middle of the night, so he had to check them out from him, as if they were a book from Joey's library. And he only got the right to do that when his ranch chores were done.

"You shoulda stayed home and played your silly game, weirdo. I'm gonna kick your ass." The boy he'd picked out as the likely first aggressor, Max Cortez, shoved the boy in the sweatshirt, who stumbled backward and fell to the ground. The bigger boy's right leg shifted, as if to deliver the promised kick. "Then I'm gonna—Whoa!"

The startled yelp came as Sean grabbed the kid's collar. And the hood of the jacket on the kid he'd judged next most likely to lay a hand on their hapless victim. The three other boys spun around, but wisely didn't move. He recognized one of them, the Garrett kid. And he recognized the boy's expression; he didn't like being here, but he'd been accepted by the cool kids. Sean could have told him it wouldn't last, but right now he had to focus on the situation. At least, he wouldn't have to worry about Chris Garrett; when Taya heard about this the kid would find out just how his mother felt about bullies.

"Well now, haven't y'all just made it worth my time to come to work today," he drawled.

"Shit," one of the other kids muttered in recognition, "it's a cop."

"A Highwater cop," Taya Garrett's son groaned, more audibly. The upside and downside of being part of a well-known family in Last Stand: even in plain clothes they knew who you were.

"It is," Sean agreed genially. "And you are now in custody for assault."

"Assault?" the ringleader yelped again. "I barely touched him!"

"You didn't have to touch him at all."

"What?" the other boy he had a grip on exclaimed.

"Texas Penal Code section 22.01, Section A, Subsection 2. A person commits assault if he intentionally or knowingly threatens another with imminent bodily injury." He added helpfully, "Following through isn't required."

"But—"

"You, however," he said to the shover, "jumped right on

up to Subsection 3, physical contact, when you pushed him. And that's a much hotter pot of water." Of course, since they were juveniles none of the adult laws exactly applied, but he saw no reason to tell them that just now. He wanted them worried, and for as long as possible.

While he had them gaping at him, he assessed their victim with his peripheral vision. He'd gotten to his feet, so he wasn't really hurt. And no longer scared, although he was still watching warily. But also, Sean realized, with interest. He looked familiar, although Sean was fairly sure he hadn't encountered him before.

The other boys were exchanging glances. And their feet were getting restless. "Don't even think about it," Sean said.

"What?" one of the three he didn't have a hold on asked, feigning innocence. Badly.

"Running. You might be able to outrun me, since I'd have to drag these clowns with me, but there's no way you can outrun a police radio."

The feet stopped moving. It was beginning to sink in that they were really in trouble.

"Look," the ringleader said, sounding anxious for the first time, "we'll leave him alone. And we didn't really hurt him."

"Actually," Sean said rather breezily, "you're the only one who'll be charged with that, since you're the one who physically assaulted him."

The boy paled then. And went quiet.

For the first time Sean turned to look directly at their chosen victim. Warm brown eyes stared back at him. "Okay if I deputize you for a minute?"

Those eyes widened. "Me?" He gulped.

"Yeah. Just need you to get my phone out and take a picture of these clownhats." He grinned at the boy. "They're just stupid enough to try and run if I let go."

"They are stupid," the boy agreed, and when Sean moved so the boy could reach his shirt pocket he grabbed the phone, held it so Sean could press his thumb to the reader, then quickly—very quickly—figured out the camera app and snapped the shot.

"Thanks…what's your name?" Sean asked. The boy hesitated. Sean grinned purposefully. "I gotta at least know my deputy's first name."

The boy smiled, but still cast his tormentors a wary look. "Marcos," he said.

It didn't trigger any recognition for Sean, and at the moment he didn't want to push for the surname. But the kid still looked familiar. "Okay, Marcos, now we—"

He broke off when he saw a marked unit driving south on Hickory. It was barely a block to the station, but somehow he thought maybe a ride in the prisoner section of a police car might pound the lesson home. So when the unit spotted him and slowed—Ry Murdoch, he noticed, which was good because he'd fall right in with the plan—he nodded him over. And within five minutes, five extremely chastened would-be bullies were headed to the station. And their victim was actually smiling as he watched them go.

Sean turned back to the boy. "Well then, Marcos, now it's up to you."

The boy blinked. "What is?"

"What happens to them. I mean, no matter what, we're all going to visit the police station, but you have to decide which would taste sweeter, watching them carted off to juvie detention, or knowing every time they see you they're thinking about how they owe you for letting them off."

"Oh."

He looked, as Sean had suspected he might, as if the second option was more appealing. He'd have to explain to Shane the reason for the big show, but his brother would understand. He'd done the same thing a time or two when he was on the street, and successfully; he'd scared Cody Moran so straight after a similar situation that the kid was in the police academy right now.

"We do need to call somebody for you either way, though," Sean said.

"Can't I just go home?"

"I need to talk to at least one of your parents."

The brown eyes lowered. "Only got one."

"Better than none."

Marcos looked up again, a flash of...something flaring in his eyes. And his tone was angry. "My dad's dead, what's better about that?"

Ah, there it was. "That sucks. Big time."

The anger was still there. "What do you know about it?"

Driven by instinct, Sean did something he rarely did: dragged out his own history. "My mother drank herself to death when I was six, and my dad was mowed down by a truck a block from here twelve years ago. Any other questions?"

The boy gaped at him. Closed his mouth. Then opened it to say only, "I forgot."

The joy of small-town Texas, and having your life known to all. "Now, where's your mom?"

"At work."

Sean drew back slightly. "Who's watching you?"

The boy scoffed. "I don't need anyone."

Sean stifled an inward sigh. If he was dealing with a parent who left a kid this young on his own, this could get messier than he'd ever intended. "How old are you?"

"Eleven."

He looked younger. Which had probably contributed to the attack. Belatedly it occurred to Sean that the boy had said he didn't need anyone, not that there wasn't anyone. He remembered all the times he'd told his father he didn't need anyone to look out for him, usually after hearing his father assigning either Shane or Slater to do just that when he had to go somewhere.

He tried another tack. "So who got assigned to watch you, even though you don't need it?"

The boy slid him a sideways upward glance. "My gran."

"Can she come and get you?"

Marcos shook his head. "She's got the flu."

"How long ago did you leave?"

The boy shrugged. "Maybe a couple hours."

For a moment Sean just looked at him. Then, softly, because he knew this child wasn't like the others he'd just had carted away, he said, "So you gave your sick grandmother the slip and left her there to worry about you when she realizes you're gone?"

The boy gulped audibly, and he knew he'd been right. "I didn't think about it like that."

"You should have." He gestured at the boy's sweatshirt. "Life can be like a game sometimes. You have to think a few moves ahead, figure out how what you do now will affect what situation you end up in later."

The boy looked thoughtful then. "You mean like when you climb a castle wall because you think the treasure's on the other side, but it turns out to be a dragon?"

Sean couldn't help grinning. "Something like that. You saying your gran's a dragon?"

"No, but my mother can be," the boy said, looking as if he'd only now realized that he was going to be facing his dragon of a mother soon.

"Better a dragon than someone who doesn't care at all what you do."

The boy studied him for a moment. "You mean like your mom?"

Whoa. Don't underestimate this one. "Yes. Exactly like that."

"Why didn't she care?"

Feeling like he'd suddenly lost control of the situation, he muttered, "She only cared about herself."

"My mother loves me," Marcos said, with certainty.

"Then you'll get through this. Let's—"

He broke off when his cell rang. It was the department inside number, so he answered quickly. And was startled by his sister's voice; he'd forgotten she was filling in today. Usually it was Lynn, the daytime dispatcher, but on this holiday Sage was subbing. She'd graduated the police academy—Sean thought just to prove she could do it—and although she'd decided against the job in the end, she was more than competent at helping out here and there. The flexibility of a small-town department, and their big brother being the chief.

"Hey, Bro, you got the victim of this cluster of little would-be tough guys?"

"I do," he said.

"Bring him on in," Sage said. "Somebody who knows him saw what happened and told his mom, and she's already here."

Sometimes being in a small town made things easier. Except his sister's voice had held an undertone he knew all too well. "Okay, what is it?"

"Nothing. Nothing at all. Just get the kid here."

She hung up before he could call her on what he knew, just from her voice, was a flat lie. Whatever she was up to, he probably wasn't going to like it.

When they got to the station and he walked Marcos to the interview room they'd taken his mother to, it all hit him at once.

No wonder Marcos had looked familiar.

He should have pushed the kid for his last name.

He should have just taken him home.

And he was going to strangle Sage.

The waiting woman stood the moment she saw the boy.

Sean saw her look Marcos up and down as if to satisfy herself he was unhurt. The boy started to speak but stopped immediately when she held up a hand.

"We will deal with what you did to your grandmother later." Her words had a formal touch, but her deep, husky voice was enough to make him shiver. "You may think of how you will apologize to her while I speak to your defender."

Finally she looked at him. Sean stood frozen, much more intimidated than the eleven-year-old had been. Because standing before him was no dragon, but a tall, beautiful, impossibly elegant woman with long black hair up in a knot and searing dark eyes that took his breath away.

Maria Elena Valencia de la Cova.

The name he'd memorized without meaning to.

The face he'd never had a chance of forgetting.

The woman he'd been entranced by since the first time he'd ever seen her.

The day his father died.

Chapter Two

ELENA WAS CERTAIN the detective recognized her. He'd been—was shocked too strong a word?—to see her here, but there had been recognition in his eyes, too. She herself had taken a moment to register, so rarely had she seen him not wearing the black cowboy hat that he always seemed to wear. His hair was as dark as all his siblings', thick and unexpectedly a bit spiky on top. But the sunglasses that were always either on or slipped into his shirt pocket were there, and the rest of his personal uniform seemed the same: black jeans, boots, and shirt, although the shirt had white pearl snaps.

She had no doubt who he was. The boy whose life had crumbled right in front of her. The boy who had stopped being a boy in the space of a few, horrible moments.

She knew he was only thirty now, but life had etched a great deal more in his face since that day she'd first seen him. Which was no surprise, given what had happened on that day.

She remembered it so vividly, when that good, honorable man, Steven Highwater, had been tragically struck down on the street in front of Valencia's, the restaurant she had been working at then, and managed now. She had tried to help that day, but it had been too late the moment the big truck had hit him. She had still been sitting on the curb, soaked in the blood of a man she'd respected, when Sean Highwater had arrived at the scene. It had been a Thursday, two days before he was due to graduate from Creekbend High School, as she had herself five years before. She knew that because one of her cousins had been in his class.

She had never seen anyone look so shattered.

Never, until she had had to tell Marcos his father was gone. Courtesy of the treachery of a supposed ally and a roadside bomb overseas, she had become a twenty-nine-year-old widow with a five-year-old son.

It had been this Highwater's oldest brother, Shane—now the police chief as his father had been then—who had come to her to thank her on behalf of the family, for trying to help. She had gained even more respect for the man who had died when she saw how his eldest gave up his college schooling and came home to see to the family. Family was paramount to her, and she thought nothing could make clearer how well Steven Highwater had raised his.

Including the man before her now.

"Detective Highwater," she said when he didn't speak, but just stared.

He seemed to snap out of whatever held him—his own memory of that awful, bloody day, perhaps, when his family had been ripped to shreds—but before he could speak Marcos had yelped, "Detective? You're Detective Highwater, the one who solves all those cases my gran reads about?"

To his credit, Sean Highwater looked slightly embarrassed. And so she answered for him. "He is that very one, Marcos. And yet he took the time to protect you."

"Wow."

The boy sounded awed. As well he should, given the case record of this young man. Who then spoke rather abruptly. "Marcos didn't do anything wrong." He grimaced, went on. "Other than scaring his grandmother and you, I mean. None of what happened in the park was his fault. I saw the whole thing, and it was the kids we brought in who were harassing him."

"That is good to know. So he only has one thing to atone for. Or two, if you count forcing me to leave work." Marcos winced. She looked back at Sean. "Thank you for intervening, Detective. I realize stepping into a child's matter is hardly your job."

"The people of Last Stand are my job. All of them." He smiled then. "Just ask my brother."

She smiled back. His smile vanished, and she heard him take an audible breath. How very odd. "Still, you could have called someone else to deal."

"I was there. And...I've been where he was. And that was back when being a...sort of geeky kid wasn't at all cool."

Marcos gave him a startled look. "You? You couldn't ever have been a geek."

"You're right. It was 'nerd' back then. And I was. Definitely the odd one out. Don't believe me, ask my brothers. Either of them."

Another memory flashed through Elena's mind, of her

mother's sixtieth birthday in January. They had had the family gathering at Valencia's, which they had closed for the private occasion, but to the amusement of all her mother had insisted on stopping at the Last Stand Saloon for a nightcap. Not for the alcohol, she insisted—although she also said Slater Highwater made the best Tequila Sunrise in Texas because, she had informed them loftily, he made his own grenadine instead of using the fructose-loaded bottled variety—but for the history. She wanted to honor their Tejano ancestor, who had stood here with the Texians to hold off an army, on his own sixtieth birthday.

But the memory that came to her now was something she had heard that night, something the expert saloonkeeper had said about his younger brother.

Sean's been a genius with puzzles since he was four. And police cases are just another sort of puzzle. That's why he's so good at it, why he solves cases no one else can.

So she supposed it could be true that he'd been a nerd. Although looking at the man who stood before them, tall, lean-hipped, broad-shouldered with those ice-blue eyes that were a different shade than any of the other Highwaters', it was hard to picture him as anything other than the attractive, rather sexy adult male he was now.

She nearly flushed at her own thought. Where on earth had that come from?

He turned from Marcos to look at her again. With those eyes.

"We made quite a production out of this, Mrs. de la Cova," he said.

"Elena, please." At his furrowed brow she added the usual explanation. "My mother is also Maria, so I go by Elena to avoid confusion."

After a second's hesitation he nodded, but she noticed he did not speak the name when he went on. "I think those kids still may be young enough for the lesson to take. But it's up to you and Marcos what we do from here."

"Our options?" She managed to ask it steadily, although she was still inwardly a bit rattled by her unexpected reaction to him.

"We pursue it, although there's every likelihood nothing will come of it because of their age and that it was fairly minor, with no real injury done."

"Thanks to you."

Again he shrugged, the nonverbal equivalent of *Just doing my job, ma'am,* she supposed.

"Or," he went on, "we call in their parents to pick them up and hope that and the ride to the station in the back of a police car, thinking they've been arrested, is enough to take some of the bully out of them."

"Marcos?" she asked.

"Let 'em go," he muttered, staring at his toes before he looked up at Sean and added, "Like you said, that's sweeter."

The detective gave the boy a rather lopsided—and quite charming—smile. "You just think of that, every time you see them. But I suggest you stay quiet about what happened, that way they'll have a good reason to leave you alone, so you don't tell."

"You agree, then?" she asked the detective.

"I don't know their parents, so I don't know if they'll have the same effect you do, but I think we should start there."

"All right."

He bent down to where he was eye level with her son. He pulled a card out of his pocket and handed it to Marcos. "You have any more trouble with those clowns, you call me, or have someone call me." He pointed at the fierce-looking warrior depicted on the boy's sweatshirt. "I'll come down on them like him," he finished.

Marcos grinned at that, and Elena welcomed it despite the scare he'd caused both her and her mother. But she would deal with that when she got him home. Or she would leave it to her mother, who could still put the fear of God into just about anyone.

"Hey, buddy," the detective was saying now, "why don't you head down to the end of the hall, to the break room. There's a fridge in there with some Cokes and juice. Grab one—" he caught himself and glanced at her before going on "—of whatever you're allowed, and take a seat while I talk to your mom."

Marcos looked at her. She nodded, and he scampered off.

She smiled. "Very nice save, Detective."

He shrugged again, and this time his smile was a little sheepish. "I'm a little slow on the parental uptake sometimes."

She couldn't help herself, the way he put it made her laugh. But then he gave her a look serious enough that it faded. "What?"

"If any bruises or marks turn up tomorrow—I already checked him now, and he looks fine—please let me know. I'd like them documented just in case we need it later."

The thought of her little boy—for to her he was still that, and likely ever would be—hurt made her shiver. It was an effort to simply nod and say, "All right." Then she asked, "Was that really the reason for this attack? His shirt and size?"

He gave a half shake of his head. "Most of it, I think. Some things never change at that age, I'm afraid. Especially with kids who…have no imagination. They don't understand kids who do."

"I suppose I should consider it progress that it was not because of his heritage and ethnicity."

Detective Highwater went very still. "If I thought that was the motive, they'd already be on their way to juvenile detention."

She lifted a brow at him. "That was rather…vehement."

"Your family has been here as long as anyone, and longer than most. You've got an ancestor on that plaque outside the saloon. And he took a chance on this town when few did, he and his family staying on when others left after the battle. You and yours deserve the respect of Last Stand."

She stared at him. It was true her family was of some standing in town, but she hadn't expected him to even know the details, let alone state them so…passionately. And now that he had, she who was rarely at a loss for words didn't quite know what to say. Finally, she went with the simple truth.

"My thanks again, Detective Highwater. For what you did today, and what you just said."

Elena spent the walk out to her car, a chastened Marcos at her side still clutching the can of Coke, wondering exactly what the detective had meant by that "I don't know if they'll have the same effect you do" remark, and savoring what else he'd said, about her family. She thought about it until they were in the car and Marcos was belted into the passenger seat.

"He's really cool," Marcos said.

Indeed. "It was very good of him to help you."

"He really scared those guys, after they knocked me down."

"I know." Detective Highwater had orchestrated quite the show, to teach a clearly badly needed lesson. For the sake of an eleven-year-old boy.

"He even deputized me!"

She blinked at that, and as they pulled up to the red light at Main Street she looked at him. "What?"

"He deputized me, and had me take a picture of those guys. Because he had to use both hands to hang on to the worst two."

"I see."

The boy's gleeful expression faltered slightly. "He didn't like what I did, though. To Gran."

"Nor did I," she said rather sternly.

Marcos gave her a troubled look, his cinnamon brown eyes so like his father's. "I just thought about how bored I was, since I couldn't play my game while Gran was sleeping." He lowered his gaze to his hands. "I didn't think about it that way, until he said it like that. That I left Gran to worry about me, when she was sick."

One more point for the detective. Yes, the boy she remembered—that stunned, scared, heartbroken boy—had become a man. Quite a man.

The light changed, and she had to turn her attention back to driving. Which was just as well, for she had just realized something. That she had gone from thinking of him as Detective Highwater to Sean…and then back to detective again. And the change back had happened after she had had that startling reaction to him as a man.

A very sexy man.

It wasn't hard to figure out that, even subconsciously, she was distancing herself. It wasn't really a habit, because she wasn't usually attracted. To any man, so deep was her grief, even after six years.

And the thought of those years reminded her she was five years older than him, and he would no doubt be hideously embarrassed if he had any idea of how she'd reacted to him. Fortunately, those six years of pretending to be fine when inside she was crumbling had, if nothing else, polished her ability to present a calm exterior.

Chapter Three

SEAN HIGHWATER SANK into the chair at his desk. You'd think he'd run a marathon, the way his heart was hammering.

She was still the most beautiful woman he'd ever seen.

And she did the craziest things to him, without even trying.

For years after that awful day he'd tried to put her out of his mind. But those first moments when he'd gotten there and seen the debris of the accident, seen her sitting on the curb with his father's blood on her clothes, her hands, heard someone consoling her that she had tried to save him, seen the tears glistening in those dark, bottomless eyes, were etched into his mind as if with sweet, searing acid. The horror and the beauty had both crashed into him so hard that it seemed they would ever be intertwined.

He had managed for a while to write it off to the overwhelming emotions of that day and the days that followed. But as the years went on, he realized that putting it out of his mind would never, ever happen. He hadn't—a fact he'd been thankful for later—gotten there in time to see his father lying dead in the street. But he had gotten there in time to see her. And she was inextricably linked to that day.

Yet at the same time she stirred him like no woman ever had. At eighteen, that hadn't been surprising. That she still did, years later, with no personal contact at all, was.

Usually he simply avoided her whenever he could. Last Stand was a small town, but not so small that avoiding someone was impossible. Of course it didn't help that he loved Tex-Mex food and her family had the best place in town for it, so in the beginning he had just dodged her work shifts.

But then she took over managing the place, and seemed to be there whenever they were open. That had been what had gotten him in trouble today, when it came down to it. Because he'd turned to asking Sage to pick him up takeout whenever she was going there, and it hadn't taken her long—she was a smart girl—to figure out why he never wanted to go himself. At first she'd written it off to that horrible day, but then one year at the rodeo parade, when Elena rode in traditional Mexican costume, looking utterly regal and untouchable, the teenaged Sage was too smart to miss the way he looked at her.

She had teased him about it at first, until she saw how seriously it had gotten to him, and realized it was all tied up in that day that had nearly destroyed their family. He supposed it was a mark of progress that Sage felt as if she could set him up as she had today. It was partly his own fault, for never asking the kid his last name. And since he'd been so proficient at avoiding Elena de la Cova, he'd had no idea what her son looked like these days.

De la Cova. Yeah, don't forget that, Highwater. She was married to a freaking hero who died fighting for his country. And by all accounts she still mourned him. He believed it, given he never saw her—which he couldn't avoid in Last Stand, although he'd managed to keep it at a distance—wearing anything but black.

Not that she didn't look incredible in it. He'd gotten a glimpse of her at Minna Herdmann's birthday gathering, before the accident that had marred that day, and the apparently common feminine phrase "little black dress" suddenly made sense to him. Because the little black dress she wore that day about took the top of his head off. There had been nothing overtly sexy about it, it hadn't been particularly short, or low-cut, but it had fit her tall, graceful body like a glove, and the high heels she'd worn curved her legs in a way that had sent him to the bar looking for a tequila shooter. Something, anything to combat the fire that burst to life in him every time he saw her.

And if there was anything more laughable than the nerdy kid she made him feel like yearning after the unattainable queen, he couldn't think of it.

"Why is our sister sitting in dispatch grinning her head off?"

Sean blinked, came out of his pitiful reverie to look at his brother, who was leaning against the doorjamb, legs crossed at the ankles.

"How would I know?" he answered, although he knew perfectly well.

"She said to ask you."

"What are you even doing here? I thought you and Lily were headed for San Antonio to see her mom."

"We are. I just stopped in to check on things."

Never let it be said the Last Stand police chief wasn't as dedicated to his job as anyone else on the department. More than once he'd come in to work a beat, or even answer phones to give someone else a day off they needed for something special or urgent. Sean was here himself for that reason, to give two of the other detectives with family visiting for the holiday the day off, but he would bet there weren't many chiefs who would do it.

"And," Shane added with a poorly disguised grin, "to drop off this info from Fort Worth for you. They're looking forward to your visit in three weeks."

"Damn." He'd been hoping something would save him. Giving a seminar might not be at the top of his I-don't-ever-want-to-do-that list, but it was definitely in the top five. But the department there seemed determined to have him after he'd tracked down the robbery/homicide suspect they'd spent weeks searching for.

"We'll try and survive without you for three days," Shane teased.

Sean made a face at him. "Why don't you go see if you can end up in another viral video?"

He figured that was a good way to cut this short; Shane was still irked that a video taken during the rodeo this year, of him putting on a blistering calf-roping performance, had hit the internet. Sean suspected Slater, given the new peace between them thanks to Joey. It had gone viral just like the others that had already given the police chief of Last Stand a fame—and sex-symbol status—he'd never wanted.

"Smartass. Watch it or I'll move you over to traffic."

Sean shrugged. In a way, traffic accidents were puzzles too, and sometimes figuring them out, exactly what had happened and how, the points of impact and the contributing factors, was fascinating.

"Maybe writing parking tickets," Shane said, upping the threat Sean knew he would never follow through on.

"Yeah, yeah. Hit the road, will ya?"

Shane grinned at him before he turned and headed out. Sean watched his brother go, mulling over the new lightness in his step. Shane had always been so serious—as if he'd had any choice—but now... Sean would always be grateful to Lily Jones for giving his brother the happiness he'd missed out on when he'd had to step into their father's sizeable boots.

And now of course there was Slater and Joey to be happy for. He found it faintly amusing that his most brilliant brother hadn't seen what the rest of them had known for a long time, that Joey was the perfect match for him. She was the only one who could keep up with his mind leaps, or who could match him quotation for quotation, the only one outside of his family that Slater had ever looked at with unfailing interest rather than one-step-back amusement. And Joey had awakened them all to something they should have realized long ago, that they were, albeit unintentionally, causing their little sister great pain.

And that thought brought him to the one thing that was

always able to distract him from the thing he most needed distracting from. The thing Joey and Slater had discovered, which the cops in the family had not. The clue that had been a step further on the trail of the other missing piece of the Highwater family.

Kane.

Grasping at the diversion, he checked his email again, even though he'd checked it this morning and it was the day after Thanksgiving and the likelihood of anything having hit wasn't even within spitting distance of slim. And he was right; there was nothing on the APB he'd put out monthly since they'd gotten that license number from the campground near the Grand Canyon. Slater and Joey had discovered, thanks to her prodigious memory, that their missing brother had gone there when he'd taken off the day their father had been killed.

He didn't do it.

Sean didn't care about the rumors—one letter off from tumors for a reason, he'd always thought—or who believed them, didn't care what anyone thought except his family. And they all refused to accept the possibility that their father's death had been anything other than an accident.

But they had also refused to talk about Kane, knowing how close he and Sage had been. They'd thought they were protecting her from even more pain, but it had taken Joey to show them they'd been hurting her instead.

Unexpectedly, he found himself smiling as he thought of the family meeting Slater had called. All of them except Sage, including Lily and Joey, had been gathered at the big kitchen table as usual, while Slater explained. Sean guessed Shane had felt the same churning in his gut as Sean had when the truth of what Joey had figured out hit them, and when Sage had come in from the barn shortly after, their apologies had been so heartfelt that she hadn't even teased them about it. Instead, his irrepressible, fierce little sister had burst into tears, pounding home just how right Joey had been. And later, when he'd seen her in the den holding Kane's abandoned guitar as she often did, no doubt remembering the days when his beautiful voice had filled that room with music, she'd been smiling instead of crying.

They owed Sage for that. Enough that he might even forgive her for the little stunt she'd perpetrated today. After all, it was over now, and now he could go back to avoiding the one woman in all of Last Stand who made him feel like that nerdy kid longing for the regal, royal heroine of his imagination's fantasy.

ELENA LEFT HER mother to put the bow on Marcos's chastisement for the day. She'd already delivered her verdict; he would be going with her tomorrow to the tree trimming at the Corbyn mansion, and he would wear his suit and tie when he did. When his grandmother had not felt up to going, he had been delighted to think he would escape spending a couple of hours in those clothes, with mostly adults having boring adult conversations, having to be on his best behavior. She had considered simply making him stay in the house, but she knew he wouldn't see that as punishment if he could play his games, and she didn't want to make her still not quite well mother enforce a ban on it.

"You've shown you can't be trusted to look after your grandmother," she'd told him. "And so you will go with me."

"But—"

"No buts. It will take some time for you to prove yourself worthy of that trust again."

The boy had flushed, and she knew the lesson had reached him. She hated being harsh with him—she'd always intended to be the kind of loving mother her child would run to for anything—but life had had other plans for her. At least the ache she felt now when she was so missing Enrique's steady hand for their son was a manageable one, not the tearing, ripping agony it had once been. Not that it was not still that powerful on occasion, it was merely that it was no longer clawing at her every moment of every day.

Her family had gotten her through it. Marcos had no shortage of male influence in his life. Her cousin Esteban—despite the fact that he was an incurable ladies' man—in particular had stepped up when needed. But she couldn't turn to him every time she needed help with her son, especially in this matter that had ended up much less seriously than it could have.

Thanks to Sean Highwater.

She allowed herself a moment to consider again the man he had become. That he had chosen the approach he had, that he had delivered a lesson instead of pure punishment to those bullies and, in a more subtle way a different lesson to Marcos, said a great deal to her. True, she knew it was in part because of the tone set for his department by Chief Highwater, but this had seemed instinctive, as if in this way the detective was cut from the same cloth as his brother.

Both brought up by the man who died in my arms.

And in that moment she was glad she had the Corbyn tree trimming to look forward to. Death had touched her life too often. It would be nice to celebrate a birth for a change.

Chapter Four

SEAN STOOD IN front of his bathroom mirror, contemplating giving up on the string tie and going for a bolo instead. And wishing he didn't have to do this at all. But he knew he had to put in an appearance. Not because of his job, but because he was a Highwater. The Corbyns were a very prominent family. The patriarch ran the bank in town, and they commanded respect just as, in a different way, the Highwaters did.

That didn't mean he was looking forward to it. One thing that had never changed since he was a child was that he was not comfortable in large groups of people. It didn't bother him among strangers, like at a ball game or a movie or a concert, but large groups of people who knew him and who he would be expected to interact with? Way, way down on his list of things he wanted to spend time doing.

He'd spent way too much time already today trying to decide how he could get away with the least amount of that interaction. Go early, when there might be fewer people? But then he'd be expected to chat—God, he hated that word—with everybody who was there. So go later, when everybody was well into whatever socializing they were doing, and he could slip in and out without getting sucked into anything sideways? But then the crowd would be bigger, pressing in on him by sheer numbers.

In between, then. Maybe, if he was really lucky, he could hit the sweet spot between the two, not so few people he'd be expected to make contact with every one of them, but not so many that he started to feel twitchy.

Not for the first time he envied Shane's ease with people. That was one of the things people always said about him, that he was so approachable. And Slater was just amused by it all, and somehow managed to stay that half-step back. As for his sister, she seemed to genuinely enjoy gatherings like this. She joked that after days spent trying to fathom the equine mind, it was nice to talk to creatures who could talk back.

His family, at least, understood that this was not the easiest thing for him, and they wouldn't come down on him if he dodged out as soon as he could. Neither would his friends. The others…well, they'd think what they always had; he was the odd Highwater, the one who was a bit different. When he'd been a kid that had been embarrassing. But now, thanks to Shane, it had put him where he was, in the absolutely perfect job for the way his mind worked. And there he'd gained a reputation that gave him respect, even among those who thought him a degree or two off.

His thoughts had distracted him just enough, and he got the string tie to where it hung neatly instead of looking like a five-year-old had done it. But even as that five-year-old, focusing too much—sometimes to the exclusion of all else—

had been his MO. As Shane said, sometimes he'd worried at things until they were trickier than they needed to be. And Slater had sat him down one day and explained Occam's razor to him.

"You can do both, Bro," Slater had said. "Go for the simplest answer because it's usually the right one, but if it's not, you've got the kind of brain that can follow the most tangled paths."

Even Sage, smarter about people than he at only twelve, had contributed. "Sometimes you just need to take a step back. Think about something else for a while."

He'd taken the advice of all three to heart, and it had helped make him what he was today. He considered his near perfect clearance rate a tribute to his family as much as to himself.

As it turned out, his visit to the annual tree trimming was both easier and much, much more tense—for him, at least—than he could have imagined. Easier because he hit it just right, with a number of people he could deal with but not so few it would be noticeable if he didn't talk to them all, and worse because on his way out he spotted Marcos de la Cova. Which meant his mother was here somewhere.

But he was distracted from that thought when he realized the boy was rather nervously peeking around the big shrub he was behind. As if he were hiding from something. Or someone.

Sean scanned the gathering, saw no sign of the boy's earlier tormentors. But that didn't mean he hadn't acquired a new set; he knew from personal experience that certain types of kids simply couldn't resist going after a different type of kid.

Acting on instinct and those memories, he dodged behind the bush himself. Marcos whirled, startled.

"Hey, Marcos. Guess we both had the same idea about the best place to hide," Sean said.

The boy stared at him. Clearly recognized him; his attire for this occasion wasn't that different. He'd only added the tie and a more formal jacket. Items that would see more action in the next five weeks than the entire rest of the year.

"What are you hiding from?"

The boy put some emphasis on the "you" as if he couldn't believe Sean would be hiding from anything. Or more likely a police officer; Sean didn't consider himself particularly intimidating, beyond his six-foot height and fairly solid build. At least, not compared to Shane. But thanks to his oldest brother, he'd been able to handle himself since he'd been Marcos's age and had come home with a bloody nose and a black eye. The then fifteen-year-old Shane had been ready to take on the bullies himself, but Sean had stopped him.

I don't want you to fight them for me.

What do you want?

I want you to teach me how to fight them.

Shane had studied him for a moment. Sean knew he'd been a lightweight, small for his age, and he'd half expected Shane to say he was too wimpy to fight. But he'd underestimated his brother's ability to rise to a challenge.

I'll teach you. But it won't just be fighting, because to fight you have to be fit, and you're not.

And suddenly he had a reason, beyond his father's orders that he do his share of the ranch chores, to spend less time tethered to his beloved games.

He yanked himself out of the memories as he realized Marcos was still looking at him for an answer to what he was hiding from. He dropped down to sit on the ground, still behind the wide, sheltering plant.

"People," he answered honestly. "Too many of them in one place make me feel crowded, and I get edgy."

"Me, too," the boy said, almost in a whisper, as if it were something to be ashamed of.

"Worse," Sean said, "they want to talk to me." Marcos's eyes widened. As if Sean had spoken his very thought. And it seemed to stun him enough that the boy sat down next to him. And so he went on. "I kind of live in my head. My brother Shane says as a kid I was really smart, but frequently surprised that there were other people in the world who sometimes spoke to me."

Sean recognized the stare of a kindred spirit who had thought he was the only one of his kind in the world. "Really?" Marcos whispered.

Sean nodded. And whispered back conspiratorially, "And sometimes it still surprises me."

That got him a rather shy smile. Followed by a startlingly adult, assessing look. "You're big and strong, though. Nobody would hassle you."

"I wasn't always," Sean said. "I was small, as a kid. I shot up six inches one year." Marcos looked hopeful at that. "As for strong, Shane took care of that. He taught me to defend myself, when I was your age."

The boy's eyes widened again. "That's...he's the police chief, right? He's big."

Sean nodded. "He was then, too. And four years older than me. But he taught me until I could take him down at least half the time."

Marcos's jaw dropped. "You could beat him? When you were my age?"

"Still can, on a good day," Sean said with a grin. Then, carefully, he added, "You might want to think about that. Learning to defend yourself, I mean. There are ways that don't take size, just fitness and brains. That's what Shane taught me."

"Would you teach me?" The words burst from the boy as if he were afraid if he didn't get them out in a rush he'd chicken out. Sean remembered the feeling.

"There are better teachers around," he began, but stopped when Marcos shook his head almost fiercely.

"No. I want you."

It was understandable, Sean told himself, after what had happened yesterday that the boy would want the person who'd helped him. But he couldn't deny the words warmed him in a way he wasn't used to. Sort of like when he used to help Kane when they were little, and his brother had looked up at him with that same sort of expression.

With the ease of long practice he shoved Kane back into the compartment of his mind where that case lived. Sometimes he simply had to think about it that way, as just another case, keeping it that step back Sage had spoken of. Otherwise it became a huge, emotional tangle, complicating things and clouding clear thinking.

And speaking of emotional tangles, teaching Elena's son would come with a tangle he wasn't sure he could deal with. He tried to think of a way out of what he'd inadvertently gotten himself into.

"You need a real teacher," he began.

"You're a police officer," Marcos said, sounding a bit urgent. "My mom says your job is to help people like you did yesterday."

"Yes." *In its purest form, as I wish it always was.*

"So help me. Teach me."

Sean sucked in a deep breath. Looked at the boy sitting beside him, looking up at him with eager eyes. Marcos didn't have a father, or even a brother to teach him. And he'd lost his father much younger than Sean had.

He had a sudden feeling of inevitability. And let out that breath in a long, apprehensive sigh.

"We'll talk to your mother about it," he said, not quite believing he was really saying it.

"No! She'll say no. I can't tell her."

"Marcos—"

"She'll say no," the boy repeated. "She'll be afraid I'll get hurt."

So will I. "Aren't you?" he asked.

Marcos shook his head. "Not if I learn, so they can't hurt me worse."

He had, Sean supposed, a point. But the crux of the matter remained. "You want to sneak around again? It looks look like you didn't learn what you should have from what happened yesterday."

"That was different," the boy said stubbornly.

Sean wondered if deep down he was hoping she would say no, saving him from having to deal with her with some kind of regularity. Because he was too much of a coward to simply say no to the kid? Maybe because the kid reminded him too much of himself?

He suppressed the sigh this time.

"I can't do something like this and not tell her about it. She's your mother."

Marcos glared at him then, and scrambled to his feet. "I knew you wouldn't want to do it. You think I'm just weird like everyone does."

And before Sean could speak the boy had run, leaving him sitting there on the ground with those last words echoing in his head.

You think I'm weird like everyone does.

Words the kid Sean once was had said and thought so many times.

Chapter Five

ELENA WAS NOT panicked.

Yet.

But she'd been looking for nearly fifteen minutes now and hadn't been able to find Marcos. She did not wish to disrupt the holiday cheer the Corbyns were so good at kicking off every year, but she needed to find her son so they could get home and make sure her mother, already upset at missing this town event, was all right and resting as she should be, and not up cleaning house as she had a tendency to do, whether it needed it or not.

She checked the powder room once more, thinking he might have darted in there where he could lock the door and avoid people. He was so antisocial these days she was truly becoming concerned.

When she finally found him, in a shadowy corner of the library, ignoring all the activities over by the Christmas tree, it was clear he was sulking. When she finally got out of him what it was about, she was more than a little taken aback.

"You asked...Detective Highwater to teach you to fight?"

Just what she needed, her son getting into even more

trouble, and adding physicality into it.

"He said to defend myself," Marcos corrected, although it sounded reluctant. "But it's the same thing, kind of."

"Not quite," she said.

"Doesn't matter." Marcos glared at her mutinously. "I wanted it to be secret but he said we had to ask you. I told him you'd say no, 'cuz you always do. But he said he wouldn't do it without you knowing."

For the moment she set aside her concern that he would hide something like that from her. "He said that?"

The boy nodded. Elena let out a sigh at her son's continuing mood, but inwardly her opinion of Detective Sean Highwater went up yet another notch.

"Stay here," she said. "I'm going to go find the detective."

Marcos looked alarmed. "You're not going to yell at him, are you? It's my fault, I asked him. He said I needed a real teacher, but I wanted him."

Elena wasn't certain what rattled her more, the vehemence in her son's voice—he had obviously quite taken to the young detective, to be so willing to take the blame—or the idea of her yelling at the man as if he were her son as well. She wasn't *that* much older than he was.

"I will not yell at him. I wish to thank him, for not allowing you to break one of the most important rules. Do you know which one?"

"I didn't lie," he said quickly.

"But you would have."

He said nothing, but she saw by the way he avoided

looking at her that he understood. And she knew he would stay put until she came for him. Perhaps he would even at least watch the activities as Emma Corbyn, the town librarian, supervised children decorating the library tree between numerous breaks for Christmas cookies.

It took Elena a while to work her way through the main room. So many people stopped her to ask after her mother, whose absence had been noted. As she spoke to them she continued to scan the room, but saw no sign of the tall young man in black. She liked that, the way he dressed, she thought. Not only because black was her own preferred choice—not always for the reasons she knew everyone thought—but because it looked very good on him. She especially liked the shirts he wore, black with the white pearl snaps and sometimes white piping in the western style.

She felt a flush of heat as she belatedly wondered when on earth she'd begun paying so much attention to what the man wore. After that awful, bloody day she'd never spoken to him, had barely seen him. If he had been avoiding her he couldn't have been scarcer. And she wouldn't blame him if he had been, with those ugly memories burned into his mind.

But she had on occasion seen him, usually from a distance. It seemed he spent a lot of time out of the detective office at the police station, and when she had seen him it appeared he was just walking the streets of Last Stand, lost in thought. She supposed it must be part of the process for him—odd perhaps, but no one could argue with a success rate that had become a bit of a legend in not just Last Stand, but the entire county, if not the state.

As she passed she made her goodbyes to her hosts and turned to continue her search. And practically collided with her quarry's younger sister.

"Mrs. de la Cova, hello!" Sage Highwater said. "Everything all right with your son?"

"It will be," she said with a smile. "Thanks to your brother."

Sage smiled, widely. "He's something, Sean is. A unique, wonderful guy."

"Actually, I was looking for him," she said, gesturing at the growing gathering. "Have you seen him?"

"You're looking for Sean?" The young woman looked oddly pleased.

For some reason Elena felt compelled to explain. "He apparently had an encounter with Marcos a while ago. I need to speak to him about it."

Sage's expression changed to a frown. "Problem?"

"Quite the opposite," Elena assured her, noting her own certainty that this girl would vehemently defend her brother if there were a problem. Steven Highwater had clearly gotten the job done before his death; even his youngest had that fierce family loyalty.

"In that case, he's out in the garden."

She thanked Sage and headed outside. It was a clear night, and she glanced up to see the array of her beloved stars, a sight that always made her smile. She went down the porch steps to continue her search. And found him standing with a teenage boy who was watching a video on his phone.

"That's so cool!" the boy exclaimed, looking up at Sean. "Thanks! Now I can get to level twenty-three."

"Helping again?" she asked as she came up beside him. He didn't jump, so she knew she hadn't startled him, but he did go very still.

"Just with an old game. He was stuck on a really tricky level, and—" was there a slight hesitation there before he went on? "—I knew there was a video that showed how to get past that point."

"Isn't that cheating?"

He turned to look at her then. There was something oddly intense in his gaze. "It would be, if the video showed how to win the whole game. But it only shows how to get past one point, the first step toward the right path. He'll have to work out the rest himself."

"I see." She considered his answer a moment before saying, "Pointing a child in the right direction is indeed different from cheating." She turned to face him. "I gather it was a game you were familiar with?"

"Yes." He gave her a smile that seemed rather surface, after that intense look. "Made by the same company as Marcos's favorite."

"So you are more than just familiar with them."

He shrugged. "If you're asking if I was one of those kids tethered to a screen, yeah, I was."

"Are there more videos like that one, for other games, that don't give it all away? Marcos gets stuck—and very frustrated—sometimes." She grimaced slightly. "As do I, over how much time he spends playing them."

"You can control that," he said.

For a moment she thought he was critiquing her parenting. But that didn't fit with what he'd joked about earlier, that he was slow on the subject. So she didn't speak, just lifted a brow in query.

"You can set a timer on the system, if he plays on a console."

"I can?" She grimaced. "I'm afraid I've had no time to learn the system, beyond limiting access to him spending money, and not allowing strangers to contact him via messaging."

"That's more than some parents do," he said. "But you can also control how long he can play, either at one time, or for the week, so if he blows through it in two days, he's stuck for five without being able to play at all. Teaches you to ration real quick."

She'd had no idea. "I can see how it would."

"And you can either give him a warning his time's up, or if that doesn't work you can set it to actually shut down on him." He gave her a wry smile. "If he's at a crucial point in a game, you'll hear about that one. Makes a heck of a bargaining chip."

"I can only imagine," she said. "And how does one do this?"

"It's in the settings. It's not too hard," he assured her.

"Define 'not too hard'," she said wryly.

He got the inference from her tone. "Well, if you know the system."

"And if I don't, I presume I have to find someone who

does?"

He seemed to hesitate again before saying, "No." He shrugged. "You already have."

She blinked. Realized what he meant. "You?"

"I could. If you wanted." He sounded awkward, as if he wasn't sure he should be doing this. "And if you trust me," he added.

"Do not think I don't know the name Highwater is practically a trust guarantee in Last Stand," she said.

He met her gaze levelly then, all hesitation gone. "Yes. It is."

His certainty warmed her. She was glad to see someone who took pride in family, who knew what it was worth.

"I would be immensely grateful if you would. Although I doubt Marcos will feel the same."

A brief grin flashed across his face. It hit her as if it had been lightning in one of the storms she loved to watch, stealing her breath for a moment. "He'll probably feel I've betrayed the gamer brotherhood."

She somehow found the air to laugh. But then, seriously, she said, "Perhaps it is not worth the risk. He likes you, and…he does not like many." She glanced around at the gathering that had become sizeable. "He especially doesn't like many at once," she added wryly.

Yet again he hesitated. She wondered if it was because he felt unqualified to comment because he was not a parent himself, or if it was…her. If something about her made him so uncertain. She wasn't sure how she felt about that. It would depend, she supposed, on the reason for it.

Finally, he spoke. "I think I understand that, Mrs. de la Cova. Because…I'm the same way. I get tense in big groups."

She stared at him. This was the simple answer to his apparent nervousness? She laughed inwardly at herself for thinking it had anything to do with her. *Self-centered much, Elena?*

"Elena, please," she said, as she had at the police station. "Is it the numbers, or the interaction?" she asked.

He looked startled. That she had guessed the reasons? "Both."

"Does it matter if it is people you know?" She thought of her huge family. "Or if you have at least met them before, perhaps one at a time?"

"That makes a difference. But I still have to seriously recharge, after."

"With…alone time?" He nodded. "That is very like Marcos."

"It's not that I don't like people, and small groups are fine, I just don't like large herds of them," he said. "I think of it this way. Some people need people around them for energy. Like that's what they draw from—other people. If they're alone too long, they lose energy. For me—and maybe Marcos—it's the opposite. Being alone is when I charge up, and being with a lot of people, and dealing with them, draws energy out of me."

He stopped, looking rather wary, as if afraid he'd talked too much. She hastened to reassure him. "This makes sense to me. It explains much I have wondered—and worried—

about my son. I must thank you yet again, Detective Highwater."

"If you really want to thank me, call me Sean." He looked then as if he wished he could slap a hand over his own mouth. She did not know why he felt so uncomfortable with her, unless it was simply that she brought back memories of a day he'd like to forget.

She gave him a wide, reassuring smile. "Only if you agree to call me Elena."

He smiled back. "I think I can do that. If I practice."

She laughed, delighted by his tone. And she found the almost sheepish way he looked at her charming.

She found a great deal about Sean Highwater charming.

Chapter Six

SEAN COULDN'T BELIEVE he'd gotten himself into this. That he'd offered to do something that would require him setting foot in her home.

Hell, he couldn't believe he was carrying on an almost normal conversation with her. Of course, it was mainly about her son, and he'd found almost any parent willing to talk about their kids.

"I wanted to thank you," she said, startling him out of his thoughts. She'd already thanked him yesterday, so he hastened to say it wasn't necessary. "I did not mean for yesterday. I meant for today. Here."

He blinked. "What?"

"You refused to help my son do something behind my back."

"Oh. That."

So Marcos had told her. And she'd come looking for him about it. This hadn't been some casual encounter resulting in that almost normal conversation; she'd had a purpose, and it only coincidentally had to do with him. He should have known.

"Yes, that," she said, and her tone was surprisingly light,

almost teasing.

"I tried to explain to him. I don't think he bought it, though. He ran off pretty pi—angry," he said, catching the cruder word before he got it completely out. She had that effect on him.

"You understand my reluctance to have my son learn to fight."

"There's a difference between fighting to fight, and knowing how to fight to defend yourself."

"I see."

He sucked in a breath, ordered his brain to focus, and chose his words carefully. "I learned for the same reason I suggested it to Marcos. My brother knew I would need it. I understand reality. The world isn't always kind, especially to those of us a half-step off."

She tilted her head slightly, looking at him curiously. "Is that how you see yourself?"

"Doesn't matter. It's how the world sees me. If I hadn't had my father and Shane, if Shane hadn't given me a shot at detective, I don't know where I'd be. Still at the mercy of those who can't accept that not everybody thinks the way they do. Like Marcos feels."

"I see."

His brow furrowed slightly. Did that mean she understood, or that she saw his weirdness just as she saw her son's? He shoved the thought aside.

"And there's more to it than just the goal, him being able to stop things like what happened yesterday before they start. Which might not have even started in the first place, because knowing you can defend yourself gives you…a confidence that shows. Shane always says if people know you can defend yourself, chances are you won't have to."

"Your brother is very wise."

"Yes, he is." He sucked in another breath and kept going. "And besides that, there's another benefit."

"Which is?"

"It will take some time. He'll need to get fit, and there would be workouts and training sessions." He gave her a sidelong look. "All of which is time he would not be in front of a screen."

For a moment she just looked at him, but then the sweetest of smiles curved her mouth. That beautiful mouth. And Sean's pulse kicked into overdrive.

"I see," she said yet again, but this time there was no doubt how she meant it. "And you would be willing to do this?"

"That's up to you. I told him he needed a real teacher, a pro, but…"

"He wanted you."

"Yes. The connection from yesterday, I guess."

"Or simply that he can sense you are a good man, Sean Highwater." For a moment he couldn't breathe. Couldn't even remember how. He just stared at her. "And he is right," she added softly.

"I…try." Well, that could have sounded more inane, but he'd have had to work at it.

"We must make this worth your while," she said. "I do not know how much such lessons cost, but—"

He threw up his hands immediately. "No. This is not something I need to be paid for."

"But it is above and beyond your duties," she said. "As is your offer to set the timer. Although given my son is not used to such activity, it seems these lessons might accomplish that goal on their own." Her smile then seemed almost…impish. An expression he never would have thought to see on this aristocratic woman's face. Then she gave him that head-tilted, curious look again. "What was it you got out of those games that made them so…imperative?"

He hadn't expected that one. And suddenly, belatedly, a correlation he should have seen long ago hit him. It was not something he easily talked about, and he especially didn't want to bring it up with her, given the past.

"Never mind, Sean," she said gently, and the sound of his name in her voice broke the dam.

"Escape," he said abruptly, aware he was staring at his boots but unable to meet those bottomless dark eyes. "The game world was something I could control. If things went sour there it was something I did or didn't do. And it wasn't the end. I just had to earn another life and then I could go on." He lifted his head then, made himself hold her gaze. "And when someone died in the game…it didn't matter. It wasn't real."

He heard her breath catch. Saw her eyes widen. "*Dios mio,*" she whispered. "I am such a fool. I did not even think of that." She reached out, laid a hand on his arm. The contact sent a jolt through him so fierce it was all he could do not to jump. "And yet again I must thank you."

"You don't need to—"

"But I do. I should have realized this was a way for him to deal with his father's death, as it was for you."

She removed her hand, and he steadied himself. "You only have a real problem if he starts to confuse the two."

"Did you?"

"No, but I was eighteen when my dad died."

"But much younger when your mother did."

It was as if the jolt of heat had never happened as the chill he always felt when this subject arose wiped it away. And when he spoke, the cold crept into his voice.

"My mother was barely a part of my life when she was here. She was only sober when she was pregnant. My father essentially raised us. Her dying didn't change much." He immediately regretted the words; this was not something he talked about. Ever.

She opened her mouth to respond, then stopped. She gave a shake of her head that made the strand of black, silken hair that had escaped the knot at the back of her head brush her cheek. "I was going to say some people should simply not have children, but Last Stand—and I personally—would be much poorer if she had not. But I am still sorry you had that burden to bear."

He met her gaze then. Held it. "I told Marcos it was much better to have a mother who cared enough to worry. I think it registered."

And again she gave him that soft, warm smile. "For someone who thinks he is slow on the parental uptake, you have quite a knack." And before he could think of anything to say—assuming he could have—her tone changed and she said briskly, "If you are truly willing to do this, we must plan."

And the next thing he knew he'd agreed to come to her house to set up the system limits on Tuesday evening after she got off work at the restaurant. They would discuss the lessons…and he would stay for dinner. He wasn't sure how that part sneaked in, but she was adamant. If he would not accept payment, she would at least feed him.

And it seemed a determined Elena de la Cova was unstoppable.

Chapter Seven

MARCOS HAD BEEN fidgety almost to the point of agitation ever since Elena had gotten home, and her mother, now thankfully over the flu, had said he'd been like that all afternoon.

"He's really coming?" he demanded for the third time.

"Yes."

"And you're going to let him teach me?"

"We will discuss the matter. I make no promises until we have." She gave her son a sideways look. "But you must leave me alone to cook or we will have no dinner tonight. Unless of course you want to help." Ignoring his look of horror, she put on her most thoughtful look. "That might impress our guest, you know, that you helped prepare dinner for him."

Marcos blinked. "He's staying for dinner?"

"Did I not say so?"

"I…don't remember."

She looked at him steadily. This was old, well-trodden ground, his habit of not paying attention. Marcos took a couple of deep breaths, his forehead furrowed as if he were thinking rapidly. Or trying to remember something. "He said—"

"He who?"

"The detective. He said his brother said when he was a kid he got surprised when other people talked to him. That's what it's like."

She set down the spoon she'd been stirring the sauce with and stared at her son. She was fascinated both by her son's unusually earnest explanation, and that Sean—there, she'd used his given name easily in her mind—had shared this with him. Clearly in an effort to help. And Marcos had responded, paying attention enough to remember this, and tell her.

"And he said he gets…edgy, he said, when there are lots of people around." She thought of Sean's quiet explanation about large groups drawing energy out of him. "Like me. He thinks like me," Marcos said quietly when she didn't speak. "I didn't think anyone did."

It was one of the loneliest things she'd ever heard, and it wrenched at her heart. She crossed the two feet between them and pulled her son into her arms. He seemed so small to her, and she regretted the times she'd snapped at him for not paying attention. "I did not know you felt like that. Why didn't you tell me?"

"I didn't know how to explain it."

Until Sean gave you the words.

It appeared she owed the young detective even more than she'd realized.

"YOU HAVE THE look of a Highwater."

Sean nearly forgot to remove his hat as he stared at the woman who had answered the door, and grabbed at it hastily, juggling it and the flowers Sage had insisted he bring. He'd never met Elena's mother, although he'd certainly seen her. Maria Valencia had been an institution at Creekbend High School, the teacher you both wanted and were terrified to have. He remembered even his father was impressed, once saying, "She runs a tight ship, but she knows her stuff. You'll learn more from her than anyone else."

He'd never been sure if he should be glad or sad that he'd never been assigned to her class. She taught history, and the assessment was she had a low tolerance for misbehavior, but a knack for making the subject so much more than events and dates. She had retired six years ago, unexpectedly.

And right now he felt beyond foolish, because he'd been so nervous he'd for the moment forgotten this legend was Elena's mother, and that this was her house. He noted, probably as distraction, that he was getting better at using Elena's first name, although it still unsettled him to think of her that familiarly. And as so often happened, the moment he thought of that instead, the correlation hit him.

Six years ago. When Elena's husband had been killed. Her mother must have retired to help with Marcos.

He'd met many who had or would do the same in his work, so the size of that sacrifice from a mother didn't surprise him. But it did make him feel a tug of wistfulness, of wondering what it would have been like to have a mother like that, something he'd thought long banished.

All this flashed through his mind in an instant, before it was quashed by the sudden certainty of what he was seeing. This woman was as tall as her daughter, and only the slightest bit rounder. Her hair, just as dark and piled on her head in a style that looked more time-consumingly intricate than Elena's usual simple bun, was threaded with silver she'd made no effort to hide. There were faint lines around her eyes and mouth, but her eyes were bright and clear and her mouth smiling, so the lines didn't matter. She was every bit as regal as her daughter. Or perhaps it should be the other way around; this is where Elena's bearing, her elegance came from. She would probably be—that other part of his brain made the calculation—about sixty now, around the same age his father would have been.

And she was, undeniably, beautiful.

All of this slammed through his mind like a train of berserk bumper cars, in that way that threatened to spiral out of control if he didn't rein it in. So he focused on the certainty that had hit him.

He was looking at future Elena. The resemblance was so strong even now he had no doubts. Time would have little effect; the daughter would be as beautiful as the mother.

He wasn't sure how much time had passed now, and had to make himself remember what she'd said about him looking like a Highwater.

"My sister says we're like buckskin horses—the look goes on." He groaned inwardly. Great. Now he'd just compared his family to horses. Not that they would mind, but this was a refined, dignified woman, just like her daughter.

But at his words her smile widened. "I believe they also say buckskins are as tough as wet leather," she said, and there was an absolute twinkle in her dark eyes as she said it.

And suddenly he was laughing. And that relaxed him enough to regain his manners. "I hope that holds true as well. As beauty obviously holds true in your family." He handed her the small bouquet.

She took them, and smiled even wider. "Nicely delivered. You'll do, young Highwater. Come in."

He felt as if he'd earned some sort of prize from a very exacting judge as he stepped inside.

"I hope you're feeling better?"

"Nearly recovered, although I still have an annoying tendency toward afternoon naps. Thank you for asking."

The house was a large, two-story building built of the same Hill Country limestone as the saloon, and was nearly as old. But while the exterior held on to that classic feel, inside it had obviously been updated with the times, and now felt mostly like a welcoming, modern home.

Once, he knew, it had been on the outskirts of town, but as Last Stand grew it had been overtaken and was now well within the city limits. But its impressive prominence hadn't changed, nor had the status of the family that had occupied it for nearly two centuries now. Long before he'd ever seen Maria Elena Valencia de la Cova, his father had taught him they, and other families like them, deserved the respect of all Last Stand, for it was harder for them to stand with the Texians against troops from the land where their ancestors likely were born.

"Is it him?"

The boy's call came from the back of the house, where Sean could see the glint of stainless steel that told him the kitchen had not been ignored in the modifications. There was an eagerness in the kid's voice that made Sean feel…he wasn't sure what.

"It is," his grandmother answered. An instant later Marcos appeared in the arched doorway that clearly led to the kitchen. "And this once I will forgive your yelling inside the house if you walk instead of run."

The boy slowed obediently, but there was a tension to his walking that spoke of what he really wanted to do: run across the floor of large tiles. They were, Sean noticed, in a near white to match the limestone, but bordered with smaller, intricately patterned tiles in shades of cool blue. And another memory clicked into place. Of the other Valencia family business, the one that had literally helped build Last Stand since the last stand.

"The original Valencia Tile?" he asked, studying the complex and distinctive pattern.

The older woman looked pleased. "Yes. A design hand painted by Elena's quadruple great-grandfather, original to this house."

"Beautiful, fitting, and meaningful."

She gave him a look that seemed oddly wistful. "You make me wish I'd had you in my class."

"There's a teacher or five who'd disabuse you of that notion," he said wryly.

She laughed, and Sean found himself wondering why

anyone found her intimidating. But he supposed in her classroom she had a different demeanor than in her home. And just as he was wondering if she regretted leaving, the reason for it came to a halt in front of him.

"Hey, buddy," he said with a smile.

The boy answered with an excited grin that matched the tone in his voice. "Hi, Detective Highwater."

He pondered whether to suggest the boy just call him Sean, but decided to wait. "How are you feeling?"

"Fine. Great."

The answer had come a little too quickly. "Not even a little sore? I would be, after that tumble."

The boy looked reassured. "Maybe a little." Then, hastily, "But not too sore for you to teach me!"

"Good to know, but it's still up to your mom."

"I know," Marcos said, quieter now.

"So I guess you've been on your best behavior, huh?" he asked in a conspiratorial whisper that was completely audible.

"Yeah," the boy whispered back just as loudly. "I've done my homework already and picked up my room, and I'm even setting the table."

"Can't hurt," Sean said with a grin. Marcos grinned back.

"I'll go get Mom," he said. "She's takin' forever to pick out clothes."

He dashed toward the stairs, leaving Sean wondering why on earth Elena would have any trouble deciding what to wear. Although he had had the same problem, wondering if jeans were too casual, and finally settling on simply donning a western tailored jacket over his usual black jeans and the black shirt with white piping, and adding a string tie he actually managed to tie fairly well.

"That is the happiest I've seen my grandson since his father died."

There was such a tremulous note in Mrs. Valencia's voice that Sean turned to look at her. She met his gaze, and he thought he saw the sheen of moisture in her eyes, the eyes of the most redoubtable teacher Last Stand had ever seen. And he realized that when it came to her family, she was as his father had been, as Shane still was, the caretaker, the guardian, the one who would make that sacrifice without a second thought.

"I thank you for that," she said.

"I didn't do much, Mrs.—"

He stopped when she raised a hand. "I believe you must call me Maria."

He blinked. Lowered his gaze and swallowed. "I'm not sure I can do that." He looked up again, saw her studying him. "You intimidate the he…heck out of me," he admitted.

"Your reputation is as one who does not intimidate easily, according to my daughter."

"She intimidates the heck out of me, too," he said with a slight grimace.

She studied him for a moment. And he had the feeling she was bringing thirty-plus years' experience of assessing students to bear. Finally she said softly, "But perhaps for different reasons?"

He sucked in a breath. Ran everything he'd said since she'd opened the door back through his mind. Had he betrayed something? Surely there was no way she could have guessed? Even his family didn't know—well, except for Sage, and she didn't know anything except that he thought Elena beautiful and that she greatly rattled him—he'd been crushing on her since he'd been eighteen. He'd even half-convinced himself it wasn't true, it was just that she was tangled up in all the overwhelming emotions of that day, that time in his life.

"She's coming," Marcos trumpeted from the top of the stairs. "She's just fussin' with her hair."

Picking out clothes? Fussing with her hair? For him? Or simply what she did for any guest in her home?

"Tell me," the boy's grandmother asked, "were you as loud when you were his age?"

Sean pulled his unruly mind back to reality. "Sometimes. But my dad was the loudest, when he wanted to be. He'd stand in the living room and call a family meeting without moving a foot toward whatever room anybody was in. And we'd all hear him."

"And come running?" she suggested with a smile.

"Absolutely," he said.

She seemed to hesitate, something else he never would have associated with the woman rumored to have quelled any disturbances in her classroom without even turning around. Then, her voice quiet and sincere, she said, "I admired and respected your father a great deal. He exemplified the phrase 'pillar of the community.'"

Sean didn't equivocate, for it was true. "He did. As does Shane."

"He's a bit young yet to be a pillar. And that silly Internet stuff is a problem."

His gaze narrowed slightly. "None of that is his doing. The department released that terrorist shooting video, tourists recorded the stampede and the rodeo performance, and the crash aftermath photo. And as for the hell and Highwater video—"

"He still has not learned who leaked it, I gather?"

Only then did he see the twinkle in those dark eyes so like her daughter's. And realized he'd been had. And he couldn't help grinning. "You make me wish I had been in your class."

"And I like the way you stand up for your brother. Family is everything, young Highwater."

"Yes. But could you call me Sean? Then I won't feel quite so much like I'm back in high school."

She laughed. And that was how Elena saw them when she appeared at the top of the stairs.

Sean's smile froze on his face as he stared upward. She wore her favored black, yes—a pair of leggings that were snug but not tight, and made it clear that her legs went on forever—but over them she wore a top with vertical black and white stripes that seemed to flow over her, both covering and emphasizing the tantalizingly curved shape beneath.

And her hair was still up as usual, but in a looser style. Wisps floated around her face, making him want to reach for them. For the thousandth time he wondered how long her hair really was. Tried not to picture it flowing halfway down her back in thick, dark waves. He had never seen it that way. He never would. Just as well, he could barely handle this.

She was taunting, breath-stealing, and ever and always elegant.

This was crazy. Even thinking this way was crazy. She was certainly seeing someone, even if she hadn't remarried. No woman who looked like this could possibly lack for men wanting to be close to her.

And suddenly he was eighteen again, seeing that beautiful face for the first time. He swallowed tightly, then again because the first time had hurt. And as he watched her gracefully descend the stairs, he felt a jab of an old but still familiar feeling.

He was in way over his head.

Chapter Eight

THEY WERE LAUGHING.

Elena had been so nervous, and troubled that she hadn't been ready in time to be there when he first encountered her formidable mother—why had she dithered so long over something as simple as what to wear and how her hair looked?—and here they were laughing.

Relief warred with amazement in her mind. Her mother was usually the hardest woman in the world to impress, and yet Sean Highwater had her laughing. And when her mother looked up at her, and then back to Sean, Elena would have sworn she saw…something odd in her gaze. Something almost assessing, or even approving. It wasn't her outfit, because she had seen it before.

Belatedly she realized her mother was holding a bouquet of flowers, an unexpected sight in December. But the red roses wrapped in green paper and tied with a green ribbon definitely fit the season. He had brought them? He couldn't have done anything more likely to impress her traditional mother. He—

Sean turned slightly to look up at her. His eyes widened, and she could have sworn she saw his broad chest rise as if with a quick intake of breath. And a sensation she had never expected to feel again in her life flooded her. Pleasure at the sight of a handsome man waiting for her at the bottom of the stairs. Because he was handsome, incredibly so, tall, broad-shouldered and trim, with those clear, light blue eyes, dark, thick hair, and strong, clean-shaven jaw. It had been so long it took her a moment to even recognize the feeling.

Rather sexy? Did you really think that? He's so far beyond "rather" it's... She didn't have a word for it.

"Sean," she said in acknowledgment as she reached the bottom of the stairs.

He nodded. "Elena."

"Thank you for coming to...deal with this."

"My pleasure." She saw him swallow, but his voice sounded normal when he said it.

Pleasure. How long had it been since it had been part of her life? She'd had the love of her family, took joy in watching her son grow, but this kind of feeling, this odd humming, the tingling awareness, had been absent for a very long time.

"Marcos, have you finished setting the table?"

"Not quite," the boy said, and scrambled past them to run into the kitchen. After a few steps he stopped, looked back at his grandmother with wide eyes, and walked the rest of the way.

Maria looked after the boy with an expression of loving exasperation. "I will go put these lovely roses in water." And then she followed him into the kitchen, no doubt to also supervise Marcos as she once had with Elena.

A moment of silence spun out between them before she spoke. "I have made a decision."

He blinked. "Oh?"

"If you will show me how, I will set this timer."

"I…all right. But why?"

"So that I can say it is my doing, not yours. I do not wish this to affect your…connection with him."

He studied her silently for a moment. "You've decided to let me teach him to defend himself."

She was not surprised he had guessed. He was, after all, a very good detective. "If you are still willing, and we can reach an agreement on compensation." She held up a hand when he began to protest. "This discussion is for after our meal. Please."

"Yes, ma'am—Elena."

"Let me take your coat."

The moment the words left her lips the thought of taking other items of clothing from him flooded her mind, and she felt a rush of heat that astonished her. Thankfully he wasn't looking at her as he shrugged off the western tailored jacket and by the time she took it from him and hung it on the rack near the door, she was back under control. She hoped.

SEAN WASN'T SURE what he'd expected. Some variation on the food at Valencia's, he supposed, since she managed the place. But he was pretty sure this simple roasted chicken was not on the menu. Then again, at his first bite and the delicious zing of whatever spices had been used, maybe it should be.

"There is cilantro in the rice," Maria said as he scooped some out onto his plate. She sat, he'd noticed, at the head of the table, with Marcos opposite her, while he and Elena faced each other on the sides. It was all he could do not to stare at her. Those dark, silky strands of hair, loose around her face, made his fingers itch. And when his mind ramped up into imagining it in its usual tightly pulled back, classic style, and him tugging it free, he had to look away in order to focus on what her mother had said. And told himself he'd better keep his eyes to himself if he wanted to get through this without doing something irretrievably stupid.

"Great." He gave the older woman a smile. "I don't have the 'hate it' gene."

"What's that mean?" Marcos asked.

Sean hesitated, but when Maria nodded at him he said, "Some people think whether you like cilantro or not is genetic. In your DNA."

The boy looked down at the large helping of rice on his own plate. "People don't like it?"

"Some. Crazy, huh? But it may not be their fault. It tastes different to them than it does to us."

The boy frowned. Glanced at his grandmother, then back to Sean. "Is that like *abuela* liking those nasty round, sprout things?"

Sean gave an exaggerated shudder. "Brussels sprouts? Yeah, kind of like that. You know why they smell so much when you cook 'em?"

Wide-eyed, Marcos shook his head. "Why?"

Sean whispered in that same, non-secretive way he had when they'd talked about the boy being on his best behavior. "It's a warning. So you can run and hide."

Marcos burst out laughing.

"I'll thank you not to prejudice the boy any further," Maria said, but she was smothering a laugh of her own as she did, so he didn't take it quite seriously. He risked a sideways glance at Elena. She was staring at him. Had he made her angry? She didn't look angry. More...amazed. Her gaze shifted to her mother, who said nothing but nodded. Some silent, maybe female, maybe familial communication he supposed. Like around the Highwater table, when he and Sage used to share a glance over Shane and Slater's sniping.

There was more chatter over the meal, with Marcos regularly giving him hopeful looks he guessed were related to the lessons he seemed to seriously want. Which got him thinking, even as the boy's grandmother plied him with questions about everything from his work to Texas history—on which she pronounced his knowledge adequate.

"Of course it is," Elena said at this last. "Consider who his father was." She immediately looked as if she regretted the words. "I'm sorry, it must be painful to speak of him."

Sean looked at her, finally. "Thank you," he said quietly. "It was, for a long time. But now it's nice to know he's not forgotten."

"How did he die?" Marcos asked.

So the boy didn't know the details. Before he could

speak, Elena answered. "It was a car accident."

He heard the slight emphasis she put on the last word. As if she were declaring she refused to believe or traffic in the rumors. And when she looked from her son to him, the understanding he saw in her eyes told him he'd been right.

"My dad was killed in a war," Marcos said.

"I know," Sean said softly.

"They gave him a medal," Marcos said, staring at his plate.

"Not much help when you want your dad, is it?"

"No."

"It is very hard—is it not, Sean—when your father is a hero, but he's gone?" Elena asked softly.

He wanted to look at her but he kept his gaze on Marcos. "Very. I don't know if it's harder if it happens when you're older, like I was, or when you are very young, like you were."

Marcos lifted his gaze then to Sean's face. And said, very seriously, "Maybe it's just…different."

"You know," Sean said, his voice low, gentle, "I think you're right. It's just different."

Something flashed in the boy's dark eyes, something that looked like gratitude that he'd understood.

"But I gotta say," Sean drawled, leaning back in his chair now, "that it's a pain when your big brother is a hero, too. Come on, viral videos? How much does a guy have to live up to?"

Marcos looked startled, but then he laughed. "You mean Chief Shane?"

"Exactly."

Marcos hesitated, then his words came in a rush. "I like you better. He scares me."

"Scares me sometimes, too," Sean admitted. "But in a good way. Makes me try to be better." *Not that I'll ever live up to his standard.*

"I think you are fine just as you are," Maria said firmly.

"Better than fine," Elena added quietly. "Much better."

Sean was at a total loss for anything to say. He had no idea how to react to this unexpected praise. And suddenly he was staring down at his plate much like Marcos had been, half-afraid he might be blushing.

Chapter Nine

"LET ME GO ahead with changing the system." Elena turned to look at Sean as he came into the kitchen. Carrying dishes and silverware from the table, she noticed, to be placed into the dishwasher. He saw her glance, and grinned. "I'm pretty much housebroken."

"You are a gracious guest," she corrected. "And I need to thank you yet again. That is the most outgoing and talkative Marcos has been in a very long time."

"I think it was the Brussels sprouts."

She couldn't help herself, she laughed. "I hate them, too," she whispered. "Aiyee, the smell!"

He laughed too, and she thought not for the first time what a lovely thing it was, both his laugh and the sparkle in his eyes when he did.

"What you said to him about his father, and telling him he was right..."

"He's a smart kid. Different, but smart enough to know he's different. He'll have to make his own peace with that, like I did, but he will. He just needs that base, that core, of knowing you love him and will stand by him no matter what."

She set down the glass she had been holding.

"You are not only gracious, you are a kind and wise soul, Sean Highwater."

Not to mention attractive, and far, far more than "rather" sexy.

And that he was clearly embarrassed by such praise, that it made him shyly look away, only added to his charm. For her, anyway. The fingers of the hand that had been holding the glass curled as she resisted the urge to reach up and cup his cheek. It was difficult. She wanted…no, yearned to touch him, for a sort of contact that would take this out of the realm of helpfulness and kindness.

And that she was having such thoughts, thoughts she had not had since the day two uniformed personnel, one of them a chaplain, had arrived at the door, rattled her more than she could deal with right now. Silly woman, she chastised herself. He could have any woman his own age that he wanted.

And perhaps he does.

That thought, much belated, gave her back the control she'd nearly lost.

"Why should you go ahead with the timer?" she said quickly.

He looked up, and his expression was relieved. If he'd known what she'd been thinking, he would look even more so.

"I mean let Marcos know it's me. It will make him think, weigh, decide how much he really wants these lessons. Maybe it was just a thing of that moment."

"I do not think so, since he has not stopped talking

about it since that day, but I see your point." She gave him a slight smile. "And it is a growing-up thing, having to make such decisions."

"Yes."

"All right, then. But you're wrong, you know."

"It happens," he said wryly. "But about what?"

"You would be a most excellent parent."

He gave her an intent look she couldn't interpret. Then, his voice low, he said, "Maybe I'll find out someday."

"Surely there are many women who would line up for the opportunity to help you find out. Perhaps an important one in your life right now."

She very carefully made it not a question. But he answered it as if it had been. "No. No one. And if there's a line, I'm oblivious." His mouth quirked wryly. "But then, I've been accused of that before."

"Just because you do not think of the things others obsess upon does not make you oblivious."

He blinked. Drew back slightly. Smiled, slowly, a different kind of smile than she'd seen from him before, the kind that made her think of the sun slowly rising over the hills. He lowered his gaze again, as if he were pleased, but too shy to let it show. And she found that charming as well.

Oh, yes, Elena, you are well on your way to being charmed. Foolish woman that you are.

"Thank you," he said, as if he were not used to people saying such things. Then he lifted his gaze to her again. "Same goes for Marcos." She tilted her head slightly as she looked at him quizzically. "Do you ever find yourself upset with him for not paying attention?"

This time it was she who blinked and stared. "Often."

"I used to live there," he said with a grimace. "Until my dad figured it out. That it wasn't that I wasn't paying attention, it was that I was so focused on something else, some puzzle or something, that it took me a moment to surface, to come back to reality and the present. And I think it might be the same for Marcos."

"But so often he is not doing anything at all," she said. She wanted desperately to understand her son, for she felt she could not help him become all he could be unless she did. Could the key be here, in this most unexpected man?

"I know it seems that way. But I bet he is. Like I do. It's just…it's in my head."

"You mean…lost in thought?"

"Not exactly." He stood up, not quite abruptly. "Can we…go outside for a minute?"

"Of course." She smiled as she rose. "It's a clear night, and I always like to take time to look at the stars."

"You do?" He sounded more startled than she would have expected.

"I do. I love them. And I am trying to teach Marcos how to recognize the constellations."

He gave her an oddly intense look as he held the door for her as they stepped out onto the patio. She looked up, as always, and smiled at the familiar, beloved patterns of light. Then she looked at Sean, only to find him watching her with that same intensity. But he didn't speak, and she had to understand, for Marcos's sake.

"So…it is not exactly lost in thought?"

"It's a little more complicated than that. My dad called it going down the rabbit hole." He hesitated again, as if he were unused to sharing this kind of thing. Which made it all the more special to her that he was, for Marcos's sake. "I remember once, when I was about his age, we went to the coast and I scared the heck out of everyone by getting lost on the beach. Or so they thought." He gave her that shy grin again. "Actually, they were lost, I never moved. I found a bottle washed up on the sand, the label was in some language I didn't know, and I tried to search the label for a clue, maybe a city or something, but the lettering was faded out, and I saw something that looked like a Mayan temple and I wondered if the ancient Mayans had made beer because it looked like a beer bottle and how cool would it be if that's what this was but they didn't have glass bottles, at least not the kind with a machined pattern like this so it had to be more modern, and then I thought of how sometimes people put messages in bottles and threw them into the ocean but there was nothing in this one, so it must have just fallen off a ship or boat, maybe from wherever this was and I wondered how far away it was…"

She knew she was staring at him, but she couldn't help it. He'd said it all in one, long rambling sentence, and she realized he was letting her see something deeply personal, the way his mind—and perhaps her son's—worked. How it started with something simple and, as his father had said, took off down the rabbit hole of wondering.

He stopped, shrugged. "Next thing I knew Sage was

shaking me, yelling that I was doing it again and they'd been looking for me and yelling my name for five minutes."

"That is...remarkable."

"Or weird, depending on who you ask."

Slowly she shook her head. "No. I suspect it is minds like that that solve the mysteries of the world." She smiled at him. "Or the mysteries of Last Stand."

"Maybe Marcos will solve some of those bigger ones some day."

"I'm sure to many of the victims of the crimes you solve, there is nothing bigger." Again she got that shyly pleased smile, and it pleased her in turn. Whether it was because it was just so charming, or that she had managed to bring it on she wasn't certain. "So...when I ask Marcos what he's thinking about, and he says 'Things', this is what he means? So many things, tumbling one after the other, connected and yet leading to new and unconnected things?"

"I...think so," he said, with an obviously embarrassed chuckle at the repetition of the word.

Slowly she nodded. "I think—" she put a bit of emphasis on the word purposely, while smiling back at him "—I understand. And yet again I must thank you for—"

He held up a hand and she stopped. "Please. You don't have to thank me. In a way it's a treat for me, to find someone else with the same...quirks."

"I am very sorry, Sean, if that is how you've been made to feel." She meant every word of it, and let it show.

"Not so much anymore. I'm good at what I do, and that makes a difference."

She liked that he wasn't modest about his work; he'd earned the respect he had and he did not belittle it.

When they went back inside and Marcos jumped up at Sean's presence in the living room she knew the boy had been anxiously awaiting the results of their discussion. The discussion they hadn't really had at all, at least not on the topic she had expected. Sean gave her a glance, with a lifted brow. She nodded.

"Okay, buddy," he said, crouching before where her son, so much smaller than he, sat on the couch. His tablet was in his lap, but for once she knew he hadn't been lost in it, or he wouldn't have known the moment they walked in. "You've got a decision to make."

The boy's eyes widened. "I do?"

Sean nodded. "About those lessons."

"I want them!"

"How much?"

Marcos blinked. His brow furrowed. "What do you mean?"

Sean gestured at the game controller that sat close at hand. "The hammer's coming down, Marcos. Time limits."

The boy stared at him in apparent shock. She thought about what he'd said about Marcos thinking of this as a betrayal. It seemed true. "That's why you're here?" He gave her an angry glance. "'Cuz she couldn't figure out how to do it?"

Sometimes she did not give her son enough credit for understanding adults.

"Here's the deal," Sean said quickly, before Marcos could

build up a head of steam. “There are two options. You don’t give your mom a hard time about the time limits—or try to find a way around them—and we start your lessons right away. You give her flak, we don’t start at all.”

Marcos still looked angry. Almost mutinous.

“Or,” Sean said easily, “you could really blow up on her and the whole system gets shut down for good.” She could only classify the look her son gave both of them then as horrified. “Your mom will have a password, and can grant you extra time if, say, you do really good on something, or go a long time without hassling her about it.”

“Big deal.”

“There are degrees on the timer, too…it can warn you, or it can just shut down on you, whether you’re in the middle of a battle for your life or not.”

The horror intensified.

“I get it, Marcos. Adult decisions like this are tough. But the timer’s going on no matter what, so you might as well get something out of it you want, right? And be able to keep playing just like you have been, just not as long.”

The horror faded a little, but the mutinous look lingered. “I thought you got it,” he muttered to Sean.

“I do. And think about it. Think about the challenge it adds to the game. You have to not just plan what you’re going to have to do to get to where you want to be, but you have to count time now, too, how to get there before the timer goes off. It’s like a two-front battle—you against the game and the clock.” Sean grinned at him. “It makes it even more exciting. You really, really have to focus.”

Marcos's expression shifted, finally, to curiosity. "Did someone do this to you?"

"Well, back in the olden days," he said with the slightest of drawls, and she stifled a laugh at the way he said it, as if he were eighty, not thirty, "they didn't have timers built in. So I just got unplugged and my system was locked up altogether. Then I had to wait until my dad had time to hook it up again, which usually was a week or so."

The look of horror returned, but she could sense the difference this time. It was horror at the scenario he'd presented, and Elena knew he'd succeeded in showing Marcos it could be worse.

And as she sat there watching the two of them, she could only think yet again that Sean Highwater was very, very wrong in his assessment of himself as parental material.

Chapter Ten

HE'D SURVIVED.

Crazily, those were the words that circled in Sean's mind as he drove to the station the next morning.

He'd spent nearly three hours in Elena's home last night—with Mrs. Valencia!—and survived. And more, Elena hadn't looked at him as if she thought he was too strange to be comfortable around, or as if she regretted having him come, but as if she were fascinated. Perhaps she, like her son, had thought there was no one else out there who thought like Marcos did.

And that's all it was. He'd helped her a little, at least he hoped so, to understand her son. And that made him feel it had been worth the strain of being so close to her for so long.

Although hiding the effect she has on you is something else altogether. Especially when she wanted to look at the stars...

The city crew had been busy with the town's Christmas decorations since Monday; Last Stand was in its seasonal best from the first workday of December onward. Light poles were garlanded and festooned, banners and lights and tinsel-clad wire structures stretched across Main Street every block. It gave the place, along with the covered walkways and classic storefronts an old-time Christmas look that he found oddly comforting, and tourists found attractive. Of course there was always some clown who thought it funny to try and shoot out some of the decorative ornaments, but since Shane's standing punishment for that, backed up by Judge Morales, was donating whatever skill they had to the town, be it painting city hall or repairing police units, nobody got too wound up about it.

His brother was a very wise man. Just as their father had been. Except for that one little problem of loving a woman who couldn't stay sober.

With the ease of long practice, he veered off that subject, although the subject of mothers stuck in his mind. Elena was a good mother. And her mother clearly was as well, giving up her career like that to help with Marcos. What would his family's lives been like if they'd had that kind of mother? Different, obviously, but how? Neither Elena nor her mother were a soft touch, so he doubted the rules would have been any less strict. But would there have been a softer shelter to run to, when they were little? Not that his father hadn't been compassionate, and he'd certainly been there for all of them when they needed him. But his demonstrations of affection had run more to hair-ruffling, a hearty clap on the back, and the occasional special-circumstances hug. But what would his life have been like without that? With only the female influence?

He realized as he pulled the unmarked unit he drove most of the time to a halt behind the station that he'd gotten here on autopilot again. His father had worried about that, when he'd started to drive, that he'd get lost down that rabbit hole and get into or cause an accident. But now he smiled as he remembered the day his father had admitted he'd been wrong.

All right, son. It seems that mind of yours knows exactly how much brainpower to allot the task. And as long as it stays that way, I'll shut up.

He wondered about Elena's mother, who by reputation had been such an unforgiving teacher, and how she was apparently quite different with Marcos. Had she been that way with Elena, or had the softness only come with her grandson? Had Elena learned about parenting from her? He didn't know where her father fit into the picture. He knew he had died, but wasn't sure exactly how long ago. Elena herself, he was sure, would put Marcos's well-being above all else, but as a single mother she'd had to be, perhaps, stricter than she would like. But she—

"Hey, Sean."

He snapped out of it at the hail from Mark Latham, Shane's efficient and energetic aide. "Mark. Something up?"

The young man shook his head. "Nope. Everybody appears to be getting into the Christmas spirit. I just wanted to ask you, I'm looking for a gift for my nephew. He's starting to get into gaming, and I'm not."

"Ah, the great family rift," Sean said with a grin. After ascertaining the nephew's age and interests he made a couple of suggestions, with the warning that he wasn't as current on things as he used to be.

"He says your videos still get a lot of hits, though. Or

rather TexasFlood's videos," Mark added with a grin.

Sean shrugged. "The classics do, yeah. Why I leave them up."

"I wonder how many of those loving commenters would freak if they knew you were a cop?"

"Maybe a few," Sean said with another grin. Then a thought occurred to him. "Hey, do you have the schedule for the workout room handy?" They had a small room equipped with the basics. Free weights, a couple of multi-function machines, a treadmill, and more importantly for his purposes an open space with mats, for sparring.

"Sure." Mark pulled a phone that Sean swore was twice the size of his out of his back pocket. He tapped the screen twice and asked, "Want me to beam it to you?"

"Yeah, thanks."

He scanned the calendar. There were a couple of scheduled things, one of the guys who'd been hurt last month was doing rehab, and the small group of weight lifters had their own slot. The rest was open. Most people used it either before or after their duty shifts, so he should be able to find a free spot somewhere mid-third shift. He had no idea how long this might take; Marcos was eager, but small and wiry. Kind of like he'd been.

By the time he reached his desk in the detective office he had made an entry in a free time period, and set it to recur indefinitely. But then he was faced with a decision that seemed harder than it should be. He needed to let Elena know they could start the lessons this evening. That was the simple part. Ordinarily, if it was anyone else, he'd just text them. But he felt the strangest urge to call her.

It took him a moment to realize he just wanted to hear that low, husky voice again. He thought if she ever called and left him a message, he'd save it forever, just to listen to that voice.

Maybe I should arrange that.

He nearly laughed at himself at that one. Maria Elena Valencia de la Cova, for God's sake. The thought made him feel a little too much like that odd, out-of-step kid he'd once been.

She made him feel like that kid again. But at the same time she made him feel things no kid would feel.

He went with the text.

FOR THE SECOND time in less than a week Elena found herself entering a place she'd never thought to enter at all. The Last Stand Police Department was not a huge building, yet it seemed overwhelming to her, perhaps simply because of what it stood for: law and order in Last Stand.

She had first thought they would do this at the gym across town, or some other facility, but it made sense that he would want to do this here. It would be more convenient for him, and he was doing them a favor. A very large favor. And at least she wouldn't have to worry about Marcos's safety. She tried not to hover, she did not want to be one of those mothers, but it was very difficult when sometimes all she wanted to do was cling to him because he was all she had left of the life she'd once had.

She had no idea where this room she was supposed to find was, but Sean had texted her to just ask at the desk and they'd direct her. There was already a tall, dark-haired man standing there, but he was to one side with his back to her, writing on a page on a clipboard. The uniformed woman behind the counter smiled welcomingly as she approached.

"I was told you could direct me to the workout room?" she asked, wondering if she would have to show some ID before being allowed into what she guessed was the inner sanctum. She assumed so, since—

"Mrs. de la Cova."

The man at the counter had turned, and she realized in surprise it was Chief Highwater. And rather inanely, the first thing she noticed was how different his eyes were from Sean's, a dark, almost cobalt compared to Sean's light, almost icy blue. The second thing was how imposing the man was; somehow his brother seemed more approachable to her. There could only be a couple of inches of height and maybe ten or fifteen pounds of weight difference, so it had to be in demeanor. Shane Highwater looked exactly as a police chief should, she decided.

And Sean Highwater…do *not* go there.

"Chief," she said, somewhat belatedly.

She saw realization spark in those eyes. "You're the reason for the reservation of the workout room? Something to do with what happened last Friday?"

She wasn't surprised by how quickly he put it together. He was very hands on, she knew, and all the Highwaters were smart, in varying ways. "Yes. Your br—" She caught herself, changed what she'd been about to say. "Detective Highwater is very generously teaching him to take care of himself. As," she added with a smile, "he says you once did for him."

The man smiled, a genuine, pleased smile. And suddenly he was more than approachable, and Elena relaxed. "I did. I figured I owed him for always trying to broker peace between me and Slater."

She had not known this. She knew, as did almost everyone in Last Stand, that this man and his next brother in age were often at loggerheads, but not that the even younger Sean had tried to be a peacekeeper. Somehow it did not surprise her.

"Did he?"

"He always tried. So I tried to get him to where he could stand up for himself. And he let me. Of course I had to tell him that if he didn't, in a couple of years his little sister would be able to thrash him."

Elena laughed. "And how humiliating would that be?"

"Enough, at twelve anyway. Of course now I'm not sure Sage couldn't take any one of us if she was so inclined."

"Good for her."

"Come on, I'll walk you down to the workout room."

When they reached the door he indicated, she glanced at her watch. It was a quarter to six. "S—Your brother said to pick my son up at six. I don't want to interrupt them."

"Not curious?"

"Fiercely," she admitted. "But I promised Marcos I

would not interfere."

"Sean'll let you know when it won't disrupt things for you to see." The chief studied her for a moment before adding, "He's a good man, my little brother. Or my detective. Either way."

"I know," she said quietly.

She declined his kind offer to wait in his likely more comfortable office, and when he'd gone she sat down in one of the rather institutional-looking chairs in the hallway. Only when she looked around and saw the window and counter further down, read some of the posted signs, did she realize this area also served as the waiting room for the detention area. Last Stand did not have an actual jail, but did have a couple of holding cells, and the luckier occupants were released from here rather than being taken to the county facility.

This would be where the parents of those boys who had bullied Marcos had had to wait, and she felt a flash of satisfaction at that. She only wished she had more faith that the shock would engender a change. But if it did not, it certainly wouldn't be for lack of effort on the part of Sean Highwater.

She used the few minutes she had to work on convincing herself that the man couldn't possibly be having the effect on her that she'd thought. But then the door to the room opened and that notion blew up.

He was standing there, looking down at Marcos, who was chattering excitedly. He was wearing blue athletic pants with a white stripe down the side, but it was what he wasn't wearing that had sparked every nerve in her body to alertness.

A shirt.

At least, a normal shirt. The snug tank top he was wearing no doubt made perfect sense for a workout, but all she could think as she looked at him was he had magnificent arms, strong, powerful, but not bulging like a man who did nothing but bulk up. Masculine arms, not those of a man out to impress but those of a man who worked. And then, as he turned, she realized just how snug that tank top was across the breadth of his chest, and how it clung to the trim flatness of his abdomen. If it were any tighter, she would no doubt be able to count every one of the six-pack of abs he obviously had. If not eight. She gave herself a fierce, inward shake, and tore her gaze up to his face, she hoped in the instant before he realized she was gaping at him.

She did not know how to deal with this. She'd thought this part of her dead and buried with Enrique. But as much as she'd loved him, and as loving as all aspects of their lives together had been, he had never sent her off the rails like this. No man had. It made her want more even as she retreated. She was eager, yet terrified, and the combination was exhausting. Were it not for Marcos, she would…what? Run? Hide?

But for the sake of her son, she was doomed to be in some sort of contact with him for the foreseeable future.

Chapter Eleven

ELENA SEEMED ALMOST nervous to be here. Avoiding looking around, anyway. Some people got edgy just being in this building, but he wouldn't have thought she'd be one of them. She seemed too serene, too dignified, too self-possessed to be bothered by much of anything.

She didn't look at him, either, but that only figured since Marcos was excitedly telling her about his first lesson.

"Sean and—" the boy glanced up at him "—Officer Murdoch?" At his nod, Marcos barreled on. "They showed me how it works. Sean's bigger than him, but there are tricks, ways."

"I see."

"It's okay," Marcos said hastily. "He told me to call him that. Because we're sparring partners now."

"I see."

He was really starting to hate that phrase. She seemed so tense. Unlike herself. Even her mother, who had dropped Marcos off after picking him up from school, hadn't been this on edge. In fact, she'd seemed simply interested.

This is the home of those who protect us. It is nice to see the inside.

The older woman's words had been gratifying. Elena's reaction was just...puzzling. Did the thought of any kind of fighting, even training to defend yourself, upset her that much? Or was it simply that she was afraid Marcos would be hurt? He wouldn't let that happen, and he'd thought she'd known that.

He tried for a joke. "I was going to recruit Shane so I could be the one to throw the bigger guy, but he had a meeting with the mayor."

Her dark eyes finally met his. "You would...throw the police chief?"

"I'd throw my brother," he corrected. "And he'd let me," he added with a glance at Marcos. "For this."

"You Highwaters are...remarkable."

He would have preferred something a bit more individual, but it appeared he wasn't going to get it.

"The getting strong part is hard, though," Marcos said, his grin fading for the first time. "Really hard. Weights and stuff. I'm not very good at it."

Sean reached out and put a hand on the boy's shoulder. "You'll get better. It's a process."

"Yeah," Marcos said glumly.

Sean thought of the row of obviously well-read books he'd noticed when Marcos had showed him his room at their house. "Hey," he said lightly, "if Harry had had it easy, he never would have been strong enough to beat Voldemort."

Marcos brightened. "Hey, yeah. And he started when he was eleven, too."

"Exactly. And those clowns who were bothering you are

a lot less scary than a three-headed dog."

Marcos laughed at that. And Elena smiled at him, and suddenly the world seemed to right itself.

"Do you have something else to say to the detective?" she asked pointedly.

"Oh, yeah," Marcos said hastily, "thanks."

"No prob, buddy."

"It was cool to be here and see everything." The boy grimaced. "And not have people watching me." He gave his mother a sideways glance that put her firmly in the 'don't watch me' category.

She didn't look upset by that, but he thought it wouldn't hurt to give a good reason for it. "There's a reason for doing it here, under wraps. Surprise is one of the best weapons anybody can have."

Marcos frowned slightly. "It is?"

"Yep. It can make all the difference, if you run into people who think they can pound you just because they're bigger. Surprise makes them slow to react. And that gives you an edge." He grinned. "Just imagine dumping ol' Max on his...backside and escaping before he can even lay a hand on you because he's too shocked to even throw a punch."

The boy grinned at that. "I'd like that."

"That's the goal. We're not doing this so you can beat up people, but to stop them from thinking they can do it to you. So let's just keep this a secret for now, okay? So you can spring it on 'em later if you have to."

The boy nodded enthusiastically.

"Don't forget your things," Elena said.

"Oh!"

The boy darted back into the room, Sean assumed for the small backpack he'd been carrying when he arrived, and that he'd pulled a T-shirt and sweatpants out of to change into.

"He did well," Sean said, for something to say more than anything. "He's determined, and that's half the battle right there."

"Perhaps his capacity for stubbornness will be of benefit," she said, her mouth quirking slightly in that way that spoke to him of an amusement she was trying to hide. He was glad to see it—she'd seemed so tense. He wished she wouldn't hide it at all. Her grin was glorious, and her laugh priceless.

"Sometimes it's all that gets you through." He hesitated. "He…mentioned his father today."

She looked startled. "He did?"

Sean nodded. "I think…I'm just guessing, but I think it worries him that he doesn't remember him very well."

She sighed. "He was so young."

"Yes."

"Do you remember your mother? You were about the same age, were you not, when she died?"

Well, he hadn't expected that one. *Serves you right, Highwater, for sticking your nose where it doesn't belong in personal crap.*

"Different," he muttered. "I didn't want to remember her."

It was a moment before she said softly, "I am sorry. That

you and your brothers and sister did not have the kind of mother you should have."

He gave a one-shouldered shrug. He'd always known it was general knowledge, what his mother had done to herself. "We were better off. We did all right. Dad saw to that."

"Indeed he did. You did a lot better than just all right."

And before he could read too much into her words, or the look she gave him as she spoke them, Marcos was back, clutching his pack with his school clothes trailing out of it as if he'd just hastily stuffed them into it.

"I'm starved, Mom!"

She smiled at her son. "Then we must see about dinner. I need to stop back by the restaurant, so you can have something there."

"Sean can come, right? He's hungry too."

Damn. He hadn't expected that one, either. "That's okay, Marcos," he said hastily.

"I don't think Sean likes the food there, Marcos."

Sean blinked. "What? I love Valencia's food."

"See, Mom! Let's go."

"You never come in," she said.

She'd…noticed? "I…usually have someone pick up takeout."

Suddenly her eyes widened. "I'm so sorry, Sean. I didn't think. Of course you don't want to go there. Not after…what happened right there."

He couldn't quite believe that in this instance, he hadn't even thought about that, the fact that his father had been killed practically in front of the place.

"I didn't...that's not..." He shut his mouth, gave his head a sharp shake.

"Come on," Marcos urged, clearly not understanding or caring about the adult discussion. Sean understood; at that age if he was hungry that was all that mattered.

"You would be most, most welcome," Elena said, the sincerity of it unquestionable, "but we will understand if you would rather not."

He did what he rarely did in his life, made a snap decision. "Give me fifteen minutes to clean up and I'll be over."

She gave him a smile that warmed him to the core. "Ah, the joy of being male and needing only fifteen minutes to look gorgeous. We will see you there, then."

She was gone before he could react, before he could even process what she'd said. Gorgeous? She thought he was—no, of course she meant it took her more than fifteen minutes to become gorgeous. Didn't she? Which he'd argue with her, since he thought she was always gorgeous. No, he wouldn't argue, not really. He wasn't sure he could, with her. But he would surely tell her she didn't need any minutes. Any at all.

He was still a little stunned. He was really going to Valencia's? After all this time avoiding it? No, be honest, avoiding her. And while it did have something to do with his father's death, it had just as much to do with her. Which obviously had never occurred to her. But why would it? He was just the scared kid who'd come upon her at the scene, who'd stared at his father's blood all over her, and stood in shocked silence as his world shattered around him. He'd never—

"You okay, Bro?"

He snapped out of the haze to look at Shane. "Oh. Yeah. Fine."

"Class over?" He nodded, still a little distracted. "I hear Mrs. Valencia dropped him off."

Nothing, but nothing happened in this building that got by his brother. "Yeah, she did."

"She used to freak me out, back in high school," Shane said frankly. "I always felt like I wasn't dressed up enough to be in her presence."

Sean managed a wry chuckle. "I can understand that. I never had her as a teacher, but her daughter makes me feel the same way." *Except I tangle it all up with dreams about undressing her.*

"She's a beautiful woman," Shane said, as if he were doing nothing more than observing the weather, "but she does have that same…regal sort of air."

"Exactly."

And as he thought about what he'd let himself in for with that rare impulsive decision, he could only see himself as that awkward kid in the presence of the queen.

Chapter Twelve

"HE'S HERE!"

Marcos's shout echoed through the restaurant and Elena winced. But she couldn't find it in herself to chastise the boy for breaking one of the main rules, not to disturb the diners. He'd been watching the doors anxiously, as if afraid Sean might change his mind. And he'd been chattering excitedly ever since they'd left the police station, and every other sentence seemed to be Sean this or Sean that. He seemed to her almost a normal boy excited about a normal thing, and she was so grateful for that she would forgive much.

Of course, Sean would likely say that for Marcos, this was abnormal. Because he understood so well. And bothered to explain it to her, in a way that helped her understand, too.

"You may go get him," she told her son, "*if* you do it quietly."

A few moments later Marcos returned, Sean at his heels. Not that he had any choice; the boy had grabbed his arm and was clearly pulling hard. But he stopped once they were through the swinging doors and into the back hallway.

"Now you may finish the table," she said to her son, and

he scampered off without complaint, another sign of his excitement. She finished signing the order form on the clipboard she held, capped her preferred fountain pen, and set them aside.

"I hope you do not mind," she said to Sean. "We have a family room in back where we eat when we are here so as not to disturb our patrons."

He looked oddly thoughtful, and she wondered if she had overstepped, inviting him to join them at the family table. But then he said, "I'd have thought it would be good, for them to see the family here eating the same food they're being served."

She realized he had just been considering, in a very Sean way, what she'd said. And had made a very valid observation. And she smiled at him even as she laughed inwardly at herself; he of course would not be thinking in such a way.

"We do, on occasion, for that very reason. But I have a feeling Marcos is going to be more vocal than he usually is, since he has not stopped talking since we left you."

"Is that…bad?"

He looked concerned, and Elena had reached out to touch his arm before she thought. She nearly jerked her hand back, such was the little electric shock that went through her. But he went very still, and she wondered if he had an aversion to being touched.

Or touched by her.

"No, no," she said hastily, drawing back. "It's wonderful. He is so happy, unlike I have seen in so very long. I cannot thank you enough."

"I wish," Sean said with an upward quirk of his mouth, "that you'd just consider me thanked and stop worrying about it. It's not a big deal."

That he thought what he was doing for Marcos nothing special spoke volumes about what kind of man he was.

"It is to me," she said quietly, just as Marcos darted out of the room this side of the kitchen.

"The table is done," he announced.

"Good," Sean said to the boy with a grin, "because it smells so darned good in here my stomach's about to eat itself."

Marcos laughed, such a genuine, happy, little boy laugh that her heart did a tiny leap in her chest.

"Then we must feed it," she said briskly, and led the way into the family dining room, where an array of whatever they had the most of lay steaming on plates.

"Whoa. Bigger than I expected," Sean said, looking at the table that would seat at least a dozen.

"And yet not big enough for my entire family," she said, rather wryly. He said nothing, but once more got that look on his face. And this time she asked. "What did that make you think of?"

He looked a little caught off guard. But that half-smile she liked so much curved one corner of his mouth as he looked at the table set for three. "That our table at home is growing. Shane and Lily, and Slater with Joey. We have a Sunday dinner thing, and it used to be just the four of us, but now..."

She looked at him consideringly. "And how does that

make you feel?"

He looked up at her then. "I wouldn't trade how happy they are now for anything." He said it rather fiercely. And as they sat down, she remembered what his brother had told her.

"I understand you were the peacemaker, between your two older brothers." He blinked, clearly startled. "I encountered him when I arrived this evening."

"Oh." He shrugged, as she was coming to learn he often did when confronted with something he'd done that he thought "not a big deal." She heard a faint sound that, from his sheepish look, she guessed might have been his stomach growling.

"Eat," she instructed, although Marcos had already begun, the food finally slowing his chatter.

Sean dived into the meal before them with relish, first going straight for the queso. And she noticed he wrapped fajitas in a tortilla with the ease of familiarity. At the first bite he let out a sigh of pleasure that gave her pleasure in turn. She liked a man who enjoyed his food. She liked a man who enjoyed her kind of food even more.

Face it, woman, you like this *man.*

"So you chose your role as a peacekeeper early in life, with your brothers," she began again after they'd eaten a bit.

"I just wanted them to stop fighting. It scared Sage, and it bothered...Kane." She didn't miss the hesitation before he said the name of that brother, the name that didn't fit the Highwater pattern, and now seemed so ominously appropriate, as if someone had known when he was born what was to come.

"Yet you are the one who tried to stop it."

"It scared me, too," he admitted, easily enough that she admired him for it. "So I tried. Didn't succeed much, but I tried."

"There are too few peacemakers in this world, Sean. You do so now as much as you did then. Do not undervalue it."

She meant it, deeply. She truly believed that most people lived in peace and calm because there were brave souls who stood between them and chaos. Souls like Enrique. And in a different way, Sean. Perhaps that was the simplest explanation for why she liked him; he was what she was drawn to, a man who took on the task most others would like to pretend didn't have to be done.

He scooped up and swallowed a bite of rice, seeming to savor the flavor, before saying, neutrally, "You still miss him."

His words brought her sharply out of what could have been a plunge into that maelstrom of emotion that, while not enveloping her constantly anymore, had never gone away. She doubted it ever would. But she was startled enough by his perceptiveness that she was able to fend it off. She shouldn't be surprised. He didn't get to be where he was without being able to read people.

"I will always miss him," she said, and left it at that.

"The way it should be, isn't it?" he said quietly. "The level of pain as a measure of what they meant to you?"

She stared at him. "You are a very perceptive man."

Again the shrug. She recalled again what his brother,

Slater, had said. *Sean's been a genius with puzzles four. And police cases are just another sort of puzzle.*

"Tell me," she said curiously, "are people like...puzz to you?"

He considered her question thoughtfully. She wondered now if she'd been wrong that his decision to come here tonight had been on impulse, since it seemed he did nothing, even answer a question, without pondering it.

"People are...different to me. Different from me. I've spent a lot of time learning how to figure them out, because they made no sense to me. I didn't understand for a long time that I was the odd one."

"You're not odd," she said, surprising herself with how fiercely it came out. He looked a little startled at it himself. But the smile that curved his mouth then was the sweetest, most aching thing she'd ever seen.

"But I am different," he said.

"The kind of different we could use more of," she said firmly.

She'd asked Rosalina, the Valencia hostess, for mugs of her delicious chocolate to finish the meal, thinking it better than coffee at this rather late hour. And Sean's reaction pleased her yet again. He took a long drink and closed his eyes for a moment, savoring.

"I haven't had this in far too long. It's even better than I remembered."

"You should come when everyone's here." Marcos spoke for the first time since he'd started eating; apparently the exercise had awakened a fierce appetite. "It's crazy, everybody ıghing."

y for a moment before saying, "And .that feeling? Like you need to get

ıis head. "'Cuz it's family. And I know then."

She w... as Sean nodded slowly, and again thoughtfully. That apparently made sense to him. Something to remember.

Why? It's not like he'll be coming to big family dinners.

She nearly gasped aloud, not at the thought, but at the pleasure the idea gave her. What was wrong with her? Especially when just moments ago they had been speaking of Enrique, and how much she missed him. And it was the truth—she knew she would ever and always miss him. But it had been her husband himself who had, before one of his deployments, broached the prophetic possibility that one of these times he might not come home. And he had made her promise that she would go on, live her life to the fullest, because it would be for both of them. And Marcos.

"You should come for Mom's birthday next week," Marcos said excitedly.

Dear God. Just what she would never wish for, Sean at a celebration of just how old she was. She could guess at what her expression looked like by the way Sean's gaze moved quickly to Marcos.

"I think," Sean said, picking up his water glass, "your mom would really appreciate you telling her first before you start inviting people to things."

"Oh. Yeah." Marcos looked suitably chastened. But then he looked at her beseechingly. "But he can come, right, Mom?"

"I'm sure the detective has better things to do than come to an old lady's birthday."

Sean coughed violently, his sip of water apparently having gone down the wrong way. But when she looked at him he was gaping at her.

"Old lady?" he gasped out.

"Well," she said, rather primly, "older than you."

"Five years? That's carrying old-school a bit far, isn't it? Never mind that you're the most—"

He broke off, and suddenly seemed to find his nearly empty plate the most fascinating thing in the world. And she sat there wondering exactly what he'd meant by "old-school." Because there was only one meaning that seemed to fit: the old-school idea that while an older man and younger woman was fine, the opposite was still a curiosity.

But that would only apply if there was a romantic relationship. And Sean Highwater was just a good, generous man helping a single mother with her son. And yet there had been something in his voice when he'd said that, before cutting himself off…

"The most what?" she asked quietly, suddenly needing to know the answer to that more than she'd ever needed anything.

"Everything," he said softly, still not looking at her.

Which told her a great deal. And yet nothing.

But it did give her hope.

Chapter Thirteen

"WHAT'S IT LIKE to have brothers?"

Sean let out a quiet breath of relief at the boy's seemingly out of the blue question. He hadn't been able to bring himself to meet Elena's gaze after he'd come so close to pouring out the simple fact that he'd thought her the most beautiful woman he'd ever seen since he was eighteen.

"It's...great."

"I have cousins, but I bet it's not the same."

Sean made himself focus. "No," he agreed. "It's different, growing up in the same house."

"But you said your older brothers fight."

"They used to. Not so much anymore. But that was inside stuff."

"Inside?"

Sean nodded. "If anything bad came at any of us from outside the family, all that goes away. Then it's us against them. That's when I know they've always got my back if I need them."

Marcos sighed. "I wish I had brothers. No sisters, though," the boy added, looking terrified at the very thought.

"Sisters aren't so bad. If they're raised right," he added with a grin. "Someday I'll introduce you to my sister, and you'll understand. Sage is the toughest cowgirl in Texas."

Marcos's eyes widened. "She is?"

"One of them, anyway. She can outwork, outride and outshoot most of the town guys and a lot of the ranch guys, too."

"That would be cool, a sister like that," Marcos allowed. "Maybe I will have one someday."

It took everything Sean had not to look at Elena. And he had the feeling anything he might say could be taken wrong so he said nothing. He wasn't sure he wanted to hear her response to that. Perhaps Enrique de la Cova had taken both her loyalty and her heart to the grave with him. He could understand that. She'd loved him, greatly, he knew. Perhaps she was one of those who truly only loved once in her life. Wasn't the fact that she never wore anything but black a declaration of that?

It wasn't like his parents, even though his father, too, had never remarried. He'd always figured that was more exhaustion and being gun-shy than anything else. Although as young as Sean had been—and as disconnected sometimes—he supposed his father could have had been seeing someone and he hadn't been aware of it. He'd never really thought about it. He didn't remember him ever bringing a woman to the ranch, and certainly never to the Sunday dinners. So in his little boy bubble, he'd probably assumed there was no one. But there could have been, and he well might never have noticed. Maybe he should ask Shane. He'd been ten years old, and being Shane much more likely to be aware. If—

"Rabbit hole?"

Elena's quiet question snapped him out of his reverie. "Sorry," he said automatically.

"You do not need to apologize for that," she said.

He shrugged. Damn, he did a lot of that around her. "Most people think I do."

"I do not. Your mind is what makes you who you are. And," she added with a glance at her son, "you have helped me to understand. So I owe that mind a great deal."

He really wished she would quit saying stuff like that. He didn't want her owing him.

"What was this particular rabbit hole about?"

"I was just thinking about my dad, after the mother died."

"'The' mother?"

He shrugged. "None of us really like claiming her."

"Some people do not deserve the honor," she said with a quiet understanding that made him feel…he wasn't sure what. "It is as well your heritage is not mine, then, or you would have carried her name."

He let out a wry chuckle. "My first thought, when I figured out the naming system."

"At least you bothered to figure it out."

"Good thing. I need it now."

He'd meant he needed it since he encountered it so often at work, of course. Too many didn't get it, and thought someone was lying about their name simply because the naming custom was different, and what was the last name to those of Mexican heritage didn't match what they thought should be the last name. But in truth, he'd learned the system not in school but on his own. After the day when the most awful thing in his life happened, and the most wonderful at the same time.

Then, before she could ask what exactly he'd been thinking, he looked back at Marcos. "Hey, buddy, maybe you can give me a hand."

The boy's eyes widened. "Me? Help you?"

"Yes," Sean said with a grin. "I need to figure out what to buy for the toy drive."

"You mean that thing the firefighters do, for poor kids?"

"For kids who aren't as lucky as you are, yes." Marcos looked a little startled, as if he'd never thought of himself as lucky before. "Like kids who don't have any parent or grandparent at all to love them and take care of them."

"Or who don't have a home," Elena put in, "and maybe don't even have enough food to eat sometimes."

Marcos glanced at his mother, but returned his gaze to Sean, who shrugged. Again. "Anyway, Spencer McBride is my buddy. He's a paramedic, and he kind of spearheads the thing, so I try to help every year. But all I know about are video games."

"But that's all I know about, too."

"Hmm. Good point. So maybe I need to think about a handheld like yours, then. With a couple of different games. Do you think some kid would like that on Christmas morning?" In fact, Spencer had saved that particular appeal for him, without even putting it on the Angel Tree they set up for such requests of Santa.

"Yeah!" Marcos exclaimed. Then, giving Sean a rather calculating look, he said, "I could help pick them out, maybe."

Elena laughed. Sean looked at her. "He's looking for a good excuse to go to the game store."

"Well," Sean said with a grin again, "this is a pretty good excuse."

"Yes, it is," she agreed.

"Then I can go?" Marcos asked excitedly.

"When it is convenient for Sean," she answered. Then she shifted her gaze to him. "And if that is truly what you intended."

"Sure."

"I, on the other hand," she said, "will be shopping for something a bit more little girly. I understand stuffed animals are always in demand."

"Boring," Marcos said. "I'd rather go to the game store."

"We could do it at the same time, at that shopping center just outside Whiskey River." It was out before he thought, and he finished rather lamely, "There's a game store and a kids' shop right next to each other."

"Wise planning," she said with a smile.

"Yeah," he said, still in disbelief that he'd actually made the suggestion. He had to be losing his mind.

"I've never been to that game store. Is it cool?" Marcos asked.

Sean looked back at the boy. "They've got a cutout of

your monster that's taller than me."

The boy's eyes widened. "Taller than you? Really? We gotta go, then. Right, Mom?"

"It seems…an efficient idea."

Right, Highwater. Efficient. That's what appeals to her. Doesn't she manage this place with killer efficiency?

"When can we go?" Marcos demanded excitedly. He looked at his mother. "Tomorrow after school? You're off tomorrow."

"But Sean is not," she said.

"As it happens, I have the afternoon off," he said. At her look, he shrugged. Again. "To make up for Friday. We'll all be working overtime, from the parade to the tree lighting."

She looked startled. "All?"

He nodded. "We always do."

"But I never see more police than usual."

"Plain clothes. Shane wants us there just in case, but not detracting from the mood. So we're there like any other citizen, just ready to take action if necessary." He gave her a half-smile. "Thankfully, it rarely is. And we get to enjoy it as everyone else does."

"So we can go, then?" Marcos asked, clearly impatient with the discussion.

"If you think you can remain quiet long enough for us to arrange it," Elena said, but her look and voice weren't stern but tolerantly amused. The boy subsided happily, and they worked out that they would go tomorrow afternoon.

They ended up talking about Whiskey River and how it got the name, then comparing its history to that of Last

Stand. And then somehow, he wasn't sure how, they veered onto the age-old subject of whether Texas should have remained an independent republic.

"I'm afraid my opinion varies depending on what insanity is going on at the moment," he admitted, "but there are times when I really wish we had."

She laughed. "I think that is true of any Texian at heart."

"Like Jose Valencia?" he asked, speaking of her ancestor who had been at the battle that had truly been the birth of Last Stand. "I know some of his history, like that he was originally in the Mexican army under Lieutenant Colonel Ruiz and helped build Fort Tenoxtitlan on the Brazos."

She was staring at him rather oddly. "You know this?"

"Well, yeah. And that eventually he changed sides because he hated Santa Anna and what he was doing, and that he was at the siege of Bexar with Juan Seguín. And he stayed in Last Stand after the fight, and ended up starting Valencia Tile."

She leaned back in her chair. "You already know more of my ancestor than many in my own family."

"Thank my dad."

"I often do." She gave him a smile that did crazy things to his insides. "And you learned his lessons well," she said softly.

They sat talking about various things—she seemed to be able to keep up with the weird turns his brain sometimes took, often requiring only the slightest clue to get there—until, to his shock, Rosalina appeared in the doorway to say they were closing up. A quick glance at his watch told him it was indeed ten p.m. The look of surprise on her face was gratifying somehow, as if she'd lost track of the time passing just as he had.

She looked across the table to Marcos, who sat with his head down on his arms, crossed atop the table.

"He checked out on us when we started on history, I think," Sean said with a crooked grin.

"He has had a busy day," she said. Then she looked back at Sean. "And not a moment of it spent before a screen. I thank you for that."

"I remember the day I realized I was grateful to my dad for forcing me out to work on the ranch. Otherwise I would have lost myself completely in the online and gaming world." He gave her a wry smile. "It really ticked me off then, but now I thank him every day."

For a moment she just looked at him. Then she said softly, "I am certain he would be so very proud of his children." Sean's throat tightened impossibly. She thankfully didn't wait for him to answer but turned back to her son and said, "I hate to wake him so late, but I must get him home and into bed."

"I'll get him," Sean said, standing up. "Maybe we can get him to your car without him waking up."

He leaned over and scooped Marcos up out of the chair. He'd known how light he was from their training sessions, but somehow he seemed even smaller as he lifted him now. The boy murmured something, but didn't wake. Sean settled him against his chest and then turned around. And froze.

Elena was crying. Not audibly, but there was no denying

the tears streaking down from her eyes. He forgot to breathe, afraid he'd inadvertently done something horribly wrong. But then she merely gestured at him to follow as she walked out of the family dining room and toward the back of the building. The kitchen gleamed in the dim lights that were still on as they passed through. She pulled a set of keys out and he heard the chirp of a car unlocking as they stepped through the back door. She turned and locked the back door of the restaurant.

Once he had the boy safely ensconced on the back seat, still sound asleep, he pondered for a moment offering to follow her to get him out and into the house at the other end. But without knowing why she was crying he was afraid to say anything. So instead he just edged the car's door shut as quietly as he could, then risked a glance at her. Her cheeks were still wet, although new tears seemed to have halted.

She said nothing. Simply looked at him. And then, with a look in those dark, expressive eyes he couldn't name, she leaned toward him, stretched up a little…and kissed his cheek.

And then she was gone. He watched the taillights of her car until they vanished. Slowly he reached up and touched his cheek where her lips had been. He had no idea how long he stood there before he finally made himself move. All he was sure of was that it was probably a good thing he had a couple of blocks to walk to get back to the station and his car.

Because maybe then he could talk himself out of wishing that had been an entirely different kind of kiss.

Chapter Fourteen

"THIS IS A good thing, Elena."

"What is that, Mother?" she asked, not completely focused on the woman who had stepped into her bedroom just as she was tying a drapey black and white scarf around her neck. She tucked the scarf under the cowl-neck of the sweater that was a black tweed with just enough white to pick up the white in the scarf. It dressed up her black leggings a little bit, but not too much. She'd vowed she would not dwell on what she was going to wear today, not when she was only going shopping for a good cause.

That it was with Sean Highwater was merely coincidence.

"That you are seeing that young man."

She froze in the act of reaching for the ankle boots that would complete the outfit. Slowly she turned to look at her mother.

"I am not 'seeing' him, in the sense you mean. And I'll thank you not to start that again, Mother."

"Start what?" her mother asked innocently. Too innocently.

"You know perfectly well what I mean."

"What I know perfectly well," her mother retorted sternly, "is that my beautiful daughter is too young to have given up on life. We all grieve Enrique, Elena. But he would never want you to give up on having love in your life. And I know he told you this."

Elena blinked. "You know?"

"I do. For he told me he had, and suggested I might have to be the one to push you to it."

She gaped at her mother. "You never told me this."

Suddenly her mother's entire, stern demeanor changed, and her eyes were twinkling when she said, "Perhaps I saw no hope until now."

Elena turned back to the mirror, telling herself she was merely checking her appearance, not avoiding her mother's bright gaze. But it was hard to ignore when her own pinkened cheeks were so obvious in her reflection.

"He is too young, Mother."

Maria made a dismissive noise. "Don't be silly. Are you not a modern woman to whom that does not matter? Besides, that boy has had enough pain in his life to mature him well beyond his years."

She hadn't thought about it that way. But even with that set aside, his sputtering reaction when she had referred to an "old lady's" birthday had been selfishly pleasing to her. And Enrique had been nearly two years younger than she, twenty to her twenty-one and eight months when they'd married. But she'd known, as he had, that it was right. And, to use her mother's analogy, Enrique also was mature beyond his years after a rough childhood in which it had taken all of his strength of spirit to walk the straight and narrow.

Sean had that same kind of spirit, she could not deny that. Perhaps that was why he so appealed to her.

When the knock on the door came her mother hastened ahead of her to open it. Elena groaned inwardly at what her mother might say; once she got an idea in her head it was very hard to deter her. If she was lucky, her mother would only embarrass both of them with some suggestion that she approved. If she was not, her mother would be suggesting wedding dates.

She laughed at the thought that it was Sean's spirit that so appealed to her the moment she got a look at him. He was in his usual black, but today, off duty, it was a pair of beautifully snug jeans, and tucked into them a knit, long-sleeved Henley collared shirt that clung to his abs and chest lovingly. Over this he wore a lightweight jacket, although it was a sunny afternoon.

She saw him nod respectfully to her mother—she liked that about him—and say a quiet good afternoon in a tone that matched. Then Marcos raced noisily into the room, even his grandmother's presence unable to slow him to a walk.

"Uh-oh," Sean said to him with a grin.

"Uh-oh?" Marcos asked as he skidded to a halt in front of Sean.

"When we'd get too crazy in the house we always ended up with house chores. You know, dishes, vacuuming, dusting, sweeping the porch."

Marcos wrinkled his nose fiercely. "Ew."

"Exactly. Even for me, if I have to choose between that and outside chores, I'll take outside every time."

"Like what?" Marcos asked with obvious fascination.

"Lugging hay bales and feed sacks, shoveling out stalls, cleaning up the horses who managed to find some mud to roll in. Feeding them was the most fun. And checking fence, because that meant you got to ride, at least."

Marcos's eyes had been widening with every word. "I almost forgot. You live on a ranch."

"Yep." Sean looked up then, giving her mother an apologetic glance, as if he were sorry for ignoring her beyond his initial greeting. Elena saw her mother give him a wide smile as she shook her head, indicating she took no offense.

"I've never been on a ranch," Marcos said, so wistfully it startled her. The boy had never indicated any kind of interest in such things. Was this genuine, or just part of the huge significance that anything Sean had gained in his eyes?

As if anything Sean isn't gaining huge significance to you, too?

She realized Sean was watching her as they got in the car—a small SUV with the Highwater Ranch Lone Star logo on the door—as if waiting for her to say something. Once Marcos was in the back seat and the door closed, he turned to her and said, so quietly her son couldn't hear, "In line with what I suggested to him before, I didn't invite him first and ask you later. But he's welcome to come, if you'd allow it."

For some reason the reminder that Marcos was the main reason they had spent so much time together lately, inviting

Sean everywhere and to everything, was unsettling.

She also realized what Sean was doing. "I appreciate you acknowledging my authority, although there's little doubt who has the greater influence on him right now."

"He'll get over it," Sean said. "I'm just…new."

She watched him as, after closing her door securely, he walked around to the driver's side. Only when he slid into the seat and adjusted his jacket as he did so did she realize why he was wearing it. Because she'd gotten a glimpse of the weapon in a holster clipped to his belt.

"You're never really off duty, are you?" she asked quietly.

He saw where she'd looked, shrugged. "Not really. Does it bother you?"

It did, but only in the sense that it reminded her of what he risked every day. Just as Enrique had. "That would be hypocritical of me, would it not, to criticize the sheepdog who protects the flock for having teeth?"

He smiled, and they had a pleasant conversation about many rambling things as he drove the few miles to Whiskey River. He seemed more relaxed than he had been, and she wondered if driving took just enough of his attention to relax that amazing brain of his. As for her son, he chimed in from the back seat often, sometimes with seeming non sequiturs that made no sense to her but that Sean seemed to instantly understand. She listened to them both, and felt an odd sensation welling up inside her, a sensation of her own sort of relaxation, of enjoyment, of…happiness. Rightness. As if right now, in this time and place, she was exactly where she was supposed to be.

She shook off the odd—and likely dangerous—feeling as they pulled into the parking area that served the small shopping plaza. She had never been here before, so she glanced around. At one side was an ice cream shop, at the other a gas station next to an outdoor outfitters that looked to specialize in fishing gear. In between was the game store, and as Sean had said, next to it a children's store that apparently ran from clothing to toys. She should have no trouble finding a gift for the toy drive there.

But she found herself wanting to go with them into the game store, wanting to understand the fascination this world had for them. She supposed that was part of the fascination Sean held for her; if he had truly been like Marcos as a child, so enraptured by this world of pixels and controllers, yet had grown into the man he'd become, then it gave her hope for her son.

And she realized then she'd never really answered his invitation for Marcos to visit the Highwater Ranch. At first she thought she would talk to her son, discover if he truly wanted to go. But in the next second she changed her mind; he *should* go. He needed exposure to different ways of living, and the kind that had turned out a man like Sean would clearly be a good choice.

They were greeted just inside the door by the promised, freestanding cutout of the reptilian monster from Marcos's favorite game. Marcos crowed happily and ran over to stare at it.

"I've always thought that if a T-rex and a dragon had a baby, this would be him," Sean said.

Elena looked at the fire-breathing mouth and the rather short forelegs on the creature and burst out laughing. "Exactly that!"

She looked at him in time to catch a pleased grin. Then a young woman in a store shirt, a pretty blonde who looked quite young to her, maybe early twenties at most, was greeting Sean rather effusively. "Hey, look who's here, TexasFlood himself!"

Elena blinked, trying to remember where she'd heard that nickname, as Sean looked merely embarrassed and said, "Hey, Nina."

But Marcos had whirled around. "Wait, *you're* TexasFlood? The video guy?"

It hit her then. The person who had posted those videos carefully showing only the next single step at difficult points of any number of popular games.

"That was a long time ago," he said to Marcos.

"But they're still so cool," the boy protested. And by the way her son was looking at him now, Sean had gone from merely cool status to exalted hero worship. She didn't really mind; if he was going to have an idol, he could do a lot worse.

"They are," the woman wearing the name tag that said Nina Lenz agreed. "A lot of us wish he was still doing it for the newer stuff."

Elena had investigated this video channel rather carefully before allowing Marcos to utilize it. But it was as Sean had explained that day, only the single step or trick needed to get past a sticking point. He'd just left out the little detail that the poster was him.

There were dozens of the videos, and with each one his following had grown, into the tens of thousands. She'd also read the post from the day TexasFlood had announced he was done, although he'd leave the videos up until nobody wanted them anymore. That, it seemed, had yet to happen.

"Texas*Flood*?" she asked, staring at him.

"Yeah, well," he said, clearly uncomfortable. "I was fourteen when I started. It seemed funny at the time."

"And more anonymous than Texas Highwater?"

"Yes."

Something in the way he said it made her wonder if it had been the well-known name he'd wanted to avoid, or the name's connection with law enforcement. But then she noticed the way the young woman was looking at him as he bent to talk to Marcos about whether the creature had the same number of spikes on its back as fangs in its jaws, and her heart ached from the longing she saw there.

I know how you feel, Nina.

Once more she tried to guess at the woman's age. Twenty-five, maximum, she thought. Which would make her five years younger, just as she was five years older than him.

Old-school.

That's what he'd called it. And in that moment she decided he was right. If it didn't matter that this woman was five years younger, it shouldn't matter if she was five years older. Sometimes she thought she only felt that way because of that awful image she carried, of him at eighteen, standing in the street where his father had died, while she had already been married and dealing with a soldier's life.

Of course, it only mattered at all if she had some crazy idea about getting involved with him.

And in her mind the word had a capital "I".

Chapter Fifteen

IT WAS WORTH the time and expense and then some to see the unflappable Spencer McBride do a double take when they went by to drop off the gifts for the toy drive. He'd seen Sean and smiled, waving. He'd noticed Marcos running forward, and looked puzzled.

And then he'd seen Elena and gone utterly blank. The man had come as close to gaping as he ever could.

Sean had bundled the handheld he'd chosen and the games Marcos had picked out together with a snap tie—which Marcos had been delighted to tell his mother could double as makeshift handcuffs, as they had that day when the bullies had cornered him—and given it to the boy to put in the bin. Elena had followed with the big, soft, stuffed elephant she had finally settled on.

And now he met his friend's curious gaze with a bland, uplifted brow. He was only able to pull it off because Spencer had no idea how he'd felt about Elena for twelve years.

"Your friend said the girl paramedic's name is Georgie," Marcos said when he came back from dropping their donation into the bin. "And the lady at the library is named Joey.

Why does making it end in ie or y make it a girl's name?"

Sean had no idea how to answer that, so he just said, "It doesn't, always. I mean, Sean-ie or Marcos-y sounds pretty silly, doesn't it?"

That sent the boy off into gales of laughter, which made the woman named Georgie look over and smile.

"So," Elena said as they walked back to his car, "your friend and the 'ie' named paramedic?"

Sean glanced back. "His new partner? What about them?"

"Did you not see the way he was looking at her when she was looking at Marcos?"

"I…no. What?"

Elena smiled widely. "There is more than a working relationship there, I believe. Or he wishes there to be."

Sean blinked. "Spencer? No. No way. He's the flirt to end all flirts. All the ladies fall for him, not the other way around."

"Even flirts can fall," she said with a smile. "And I have that on very good authority."

He opened both doors on the passenger side, but as Marcos scrambled into the car he kept his gaze on her, working out what she was hinting at.

"Your husband was…?"

"A flirt of the highest order. He was handsome, charming, witty—"

"And a hero. Don't forget that." *And how the hell does anyone else ever compete with that?*

"I never forget. I have a weakness for heroes, it seems."

Sean blinked. What did *that* mean? And why the hell was he standing here second-guessing everything she was saying? "As with your friend, he had any number of women trailing after him. I'm afraid I made him work quite hard to convince me he had left all that behind."

"Any man would leave more than that behind for you." *Damn, just shut up, Highwater.*

"But I would not wish for just any man," she said softly.

She was looking at him in a way that made him nervous. Edgy. Almost like he felt when he had to wade into a crowd, but different. More like heading into something he knew would be overwhelming, yet knowing he had no choice but to do it.

And that old feeling swept over him again, that he was in over his head, that he didn't belong. Didn't belong in the normal world. Didn't belong in this world where most people thought in similar ways, not following or even understanding the odd, down-the-rabbit-hole paths his mind took.

Didn't belong with her.

Elena de la Cova was far too much for the likes of him. It would take a man such as Enrique de la Cova had been to be a match for her. A full-on hero.

And he was most definitely not that.

ELENA TRIED AGAIN to rein in her unruly thoughts. With about as much luck as she'd been having since yesterday.

Even preparing for the hectic pace at the restaurant, usually busy on a Friday anyway but always chaos on the day of the Christmas Parade and the tree lighting, hadn't been enough to keep her from dwelling on what had happened yesterday.

She had read too much into what Sean had said, about what any man would do for her. And she'd been too honest, had told him of her instinctive attraction to heroes, and that she would not wish for an ordinary man. Which he was not, not by any stretch.

Face it, Elena. You scared him off.

There was no mistaking the look that had come into his eyes in that moment. The retreat. He had dodged away so quickly, both physically and mentally, that she could not possibly misunderstand.

And thus ends a foolish woman's foolish flight of fancy.

She'd read that somewhere. Had ended up reading it aloud, as she frequently did with any string of alliteration. She'd laughed at it at the time. She wasn't laughing now.

"We'll see Sean, won't we?" Marcos asked as he looked toward the front windows of the restaurant, clearly eager to see his favorite person in life just now.

"He will be there," she said. "But remember he will be working, so we cannot bother him."

"Oh." Downcast, the boy sighed. "But we can at least say hi, can't we?"

We? Doubtful. "I'm sure you can say hello to him. Now go make sure your grandmother has a seat for the parade."

Her mother insisted she was fully recovered, but that didn't mean she wanted to stand for the entire parade. They had, as they usually did, placed some chairs outside by the curb, for their older or disabled customers to use for the passing display of riders, wagons, the high school band, and of course Santa.

"A large turnout this year," her mother observed when Elena walked outside with her.

"Yes."

And Elena was cravenly glad of it; it made it less likely she would encounter Sean Highwater. He, and the rest of the Last Stand officers, would likely have their hands full dealing with the crowd. Nothing serious ever happened, but she had a feeling that was probably in large part because of their presence.

Even as she had the thought her mother spoke again, and this time in a tone of great satisfaction. "And there's your young man."

Elena went still, refused to look where her mother was indicating, scrambling in her mind for a way out of this. "Marcos? He's right here."

"Do not play dumb with me, Maria Elena. You know perfectly well what I mean."

"Was that your strict teacher voice?" she asked wryly, surrendering and turning.

"It never worked particularly well on you."

"Perhaps because you passed your stubborn along to me," she said sweetly.

Usually that earned her a comment on parental respect, but tonight it only got her a rather knowing smile. "I hope so," her mother said.

"Hey! It's Sean!" Marcos yelped and was gone before she could move. If she lost track of him in this crowd…

Before she could even begin to panic she spotted them, Sean ushering Marcos back toward them. Even over the chattering of the people in between them she could pick out his voice, telling the boy he should stick with his mom and grandmother in this crowd.

"They might need you," he was saying in all seriousness, and she saw Marcos look at her wide-eyed, as if that idea had never occurred to him. For someone who thought he had no parenting skills, the man certainly seemed to always find the right thing to say to her son.

She realized, as he walked toward them, that he wasn't in his usual unrelieved black. That he'd changed to a white western shirt with red piping, and a red string tie. A nod to the season, she guessed, and found it oddly endearing. She'd seen a few other officers she recognized on their way here, some in uniform, but more in plain clothes as Sean had said. None of them had taken that extra step with any kind of seasonal attire. Was that indicative of how he felt about the season, or just a whim?

And when have you ever spent so much time analyzing every detail of what a man says, does, and wears? Oh, and how he looks, moves, and smells deliciously like the sage his sister was named for?

Only once. And when that man had died, she'd thought that would be the end of it, for her.

And then he was there, and she felt…she wasn't sure what she felt. He nodded respectfully to her mother first.

"Mrs. Valencia. I'm glad you're well again, and outside to enjoy the evening."

"You truly must call me Maria," her mother said, smiling widely. "But I am now right as rain, as your father used to say. Thank you."

If Sean was startled by the reference he didn't show it, he just smiled. And only then did he look at her. "Elena," he said, and she felt silly for being relieved; she'd been half-afraid he'd revert to formality.

"Sean," she returned.

"Might want to stay together," he said with a look at Marcos. "We've got a lot of out-of-towners here."

"And they might not be as well behaved as we are?" she asked, managing a smile.

"Or as afraid of my brother." She saw a flash of a grin. And felt another burst of relief; whatever had happened yesterday, he apparently wasn't holding on to it.

"I don't know," she said thoughtfully. "His internet fame is rather widespread."

She got the full grin then, and it warmed her. "Much to his disgust," he said.

She grinned back, feeling so much lighter than when she'd left the house it was almost dizzying. "Were you behind that leaked video, by chance?"

He threw up his hands in mock horror. "Not me." Then, with an even better grin, he added, "But only because I didn't think of it first."

She laughed at the admission. "I like the red, by the way," she said, gesturing at his shirt and tie.

"Sage bought them for me. Said she was tired of me looking like an old black and white western movie."

She laughed again. "I like your sister. She's always so funny when she comes into the restaurant."

He looked oddly as if he were about to say something but then thought better of it and said nothing. She wondered what it had been. She was still studying his face—a habit she had gotten into with frightening ease—when someone jostled her from behind, and for an instant irritation flashed in his eyes. She saw him tamp it down as if it were a physical effort.

"Is this…difficult? The crowd?"

He shrugged. "Just annoying. It's different when I'm working. I can focus on the job that needs to be done."

And then he was excusing himself to do just that, continue on his reconnaissance disguised as a casual stroll amidst the throng.

He'd acted as if nothing had happened, as if there had never been that intense moment yesterday. They'd slid back into their easy conversation, and he'd laughed and grinned. Surely that should make her feel better?

So why was she standing here feeling as if she'd lost the chance at something rare and precious?

Chapter Sixteen

HE'D GOTTEN THROUGH it.

Sean sucked in a deep breath as he kept walking. He actually thought he'd done pretty well, all things considered.

He'd told himself before he'd come out here that he should go back to avoiding her. It had done the job for twelve years, hadn't it? Just not seeing her kept a lid on it most of the time. And he needed to put that lid back on. Because it had become clear to him he wasn't quite...sane around her. No one had ever had the effect on him that she had. She dragged out emotions in him he'd spent a lot of his life doubting he was even capable of. He, who was so adept at puzzles, utterly sucked when emotions tangled up the issue.

You don't even know how to deal with your own, let alone someone else's.

Especially hers.

The bottom line he needed to remember was that she was still mourning her dead husband. The constant black proved that, didn't it?

Well, you wear it too.

He stopped abruptly. Heard someone behind him mutter as they nearly ran into him. But he'd had a sudden memory flash through his mind, and it had stopped him in his tracks. It was vivid and sharp, of the day at the Fourth of July rodeo when he'd torn his favorite shirt during the kids' goat-tying event.

He stepped out of the crowd to stand near the doors of Last Stand Expeditions, the outdoor store, as the images flooded him. His favorite, bright red shirt. The one his father had bought for him that day when he was fourteen, and they'd gone to San Antonio so he could see the Alamo. Just him and Dad—something his father had done regularly, spending a day alone with one of his kids—and it produced some of his best memories.

Memories he rarely looked at now, because of the impossible pain of knowing that less than four years later that man who had been the rock of his life would be dead.

He hadn't made a conscious decision then, about the color. But he remembered it had started with a black shirt of his father's that he had taken to wearing after the funeral. And it felt…right. Not good, nothing felt good then, but right.

Gradually it had become a habit, one he justified by saying it made choosing what to wear so much easier; if everything was black, it all matched. And when the folly of wearing black, long-sleeved shirts in a Texas summer became obvious, he'd shifted to the white, for survival.

But now he was wondering if maybe he was just…stuck.

Nothing wrong with staying put, son. Unless you're staying because you're afraid to move.

He felt a rush of longing he hadn't experienced in a long time, a swelling wish that he could turn to the man whose wisdom had made sense of so much to him. The man who, even though he hadn't quite understood the way Sean's mind worked, had always acknowledged it and given it as much respect as the rest of his children. Maybe Dad could make sense of what he was feeling now. Hadn't he spent his life in love with a problematical woman? But then he felt a rush of remorse that he'd compared Elena to his mother in any way. Elena was strong, competent, steady, and brave, while his mother had been the opposite of all those things.

Love, he thought for at least the millionth time in his life, made no sense at all. How could a man like his father be so in love with someone like his mother that he put up with all her flaws?

He'd asked him that once, in his less than tactful, twelve-year-old way. It was the only time his father had ever given a completely unsatisfactory answer. That the heart wants what it wants had made absolutely no sense to him; didn't the brain decide what you wanted? He'd gone to Slater with that one, but his then fourteen-year-old brother had been so busy dealing with college recruiters, after him even at that age, that all he'd told Sean was that when it finally made sense to him, he'd wish it didn't.

It made sense now.

And Slater had been right; now that it did, he found himself wishing for the simpler days.

The heart wants what it wants.

He supposed he should be gratified that his heart had at least been consistent. It had always been Elena.

"Hey, Bro."

He nearly jumped at the sound of Slater's voice; it was as if his thoughts of his brother had conjured him up. He was, of course, with Joey. Because these days he was always with Joey. He gave the quiet-seeming woman with the betraying red streak in her hair a smile. He'd always worried his brilliant brother would eventually leave Last Stand again, that the town was just too small to hold his prodigious brain. But he had Joey now, who gave him a run for his money every day, and Slater had never been happier.

Seeing them together had, he had admitted one quiet night in the silence of his wing of the ranch house, even given him hope, that someday there might be someone who could deal with his oddity, and his plunges down the rabbit hole.

But the only woman who had ever stirred him beyond that faint hope was way beyond his reach.

"Figured you'd be busy at the saloon," he said. "Maybe adding Christmas music to the jukebox," he added, teasingly jabbing at his brother's aversion. People needed someplace to get a way from it, Slater always said.

His brother just smiled. "Klaus is handling things nicely for the moment."

"I forgot you hired the embodiment of Father Christmas to bartend." Sean suspected it was as much that Slater wanted more time with Joey as it was seasonal help.

"Besides, it will be busier after the tree lighting, when

everybody decides it's time for a nightcap before that cold walk home." He gave the woman beside him a loving smile. "Joey talked me into adding hot buttered rum to the menu for the season."

"Good idea," Sean said, and before he thought added, "and maybe some *ponche con piquete.*"

"What's that?" Joey asked.

"It's essentially fruit punch, served spiced and warm," Sean said. "The sting—that's the *piquete*—could be tequila, since you're already doing rum. Or leave it out, for anybody who doesn't want the alcohol."

"I'm impressed."

He froze. The quiet, all too familiar voice had come from behind him. Immediately behind him. And in the moment he realized how close she was, he realized he'd been aware of that sweet, light lavender scent in the instant before she spoke.

He managed not to whirl around like a half-cocked dervish. Barely.

"Elena!" Joey exclaimed with a wide smile, then Slater spoke with an ease Sean envied.

"Sean's our go-to on Hispanic traditions when Esteban isn't available," Slater said, referring to her cousin, whose family owned Valencia's. "Has been since he was, what, eighteen?"

"Exactly," he muttered. It had been his only distraction in those ugly days after the accident; inspired by her he'd dug deep, done lots of research, until the Mexican traditions were nearly as familiar to him as his own. It had distracted him from the pain, for short periods, and he needed that to get through. He just had to have moments when it wasn't uppermost in his mind, and that—because of the connection to her—was the only thing that had done it.

"In fact," Slater added, "the whole Tejano contingent added to the rodeo parade ten years ago, that you ride in, that was his idea."

She turned slightly, and he swore he could feel her gaze burning into him. "I had no idea," she said softly. "I thank you, for honoring our traditions as well as your own."

Sean had had about all he could take. "I need to get moving. I haven't walked the other side yet."

"Seems pretty calm," Slater said.

"I'd watch the Phelps boys in front of the Carriage House, though," Joey said. "Doesn't take much to send them off in the wrong direction."

"Thanks. I'll make sure they know we're around."

He tipped the brim of his hat to the two women, smiled as best he could, and walked away. And that he was all the way to the pet shop before he was breathing normally again was something he would just keep to himself.

The parade came off without incident, except for a flat tire on the classic old convertible that the mayor had commandeered for his pomp and circumstance ride down Main Street. The hoots and hollers that came from the sidelines were a pretty good measure of his standing in town. Or lack thereof. Just as the fact that he had to have—and expected—help changing that flat was a testament to his effectiveness in his office.

That it had been his sister Sage and Jessie McBride who went out and changed that tire had made the entire crowd roar with laughter.

The laughter changed to cheers as the Creekbend High School band marched past, followed by the mounted contingent—all the candidates for the rodeo scholarship that would be funded by the charity Christmas Ball in a couple of weeks.

When the crowd had cheered Santa's arrival, and then began to move along the street, Sean kept his eyes moving, looking for any knots of people that might turn into something other than just friends gathered after the parade. If things ran to tradition, there would be a lull in the late afternoon, then the crowd would start to build again as evening and the tree lighting drew near. Lots of people would come early, to have dinner in town before the ceremonial flipping of the switch that would light up the towering tree. Valencia's would be jammed, so it would be unlikely he would encounter Elena—

He yanked his mind off that all too familiar path, focused on his job for the rest of the day. Tonight that would be merely seeing that everyone stayed peaceful in the clearing out. Once the number out on the streets was down to a normal Friday night, he was done and could go home. Or anyplace else he could think of to get that woman out of his head.

Maybe he'd even hit the saloon; that hot buttered rum sounded pretty darned good at the moment. Certainly more potent than the hot chocolate and cookies being offered at the booths set up near the tree.

He'd never managed to drink himself into oblivion, but at this point he was willing to try.

Chapter Seventeen

THEY WERE AN interesting combination, Elena thought as she wandered the shelves of the library. Joella Douglas—or Joey, she amended, remembering with a smile the exchange between Marcos and Sean about adding ie and y to names—and the saloonkeeper. Not a pairing she would have thought of, but clearly it worked for them.

Although she guessed there was a lot of truth in what she'd heard Joey say, that for Slater it was as much the caretaking of Last Stand history as saloon keeping. That history was something that ran as deep in the Highwater family as it did in her own, and they were good stewards of it.

As Joey was a good steward of this place. It showed in the tidy shelves, the occasional clever arrangement highlighting a particular book or theme. She and Emma Corbyn were very good at what they did, and their love of it showed clearly. She thought of the books she had often seen Slater Highwater reading—print books, often hard covers, thick and sometimes ponderous-looking tomes with long titles and authors she did not recognize—and wondered if that was what had drawn Joey to him. Not that those Highwater looks weren't enough, but Joey seemed to her the personification of still waters, and Elena suspected it would take much more than surface things to hold her.

Whatever the connection was between them, it was clearly strong. And obvious, as it had been yesterday at the festivities.

"It seems you are always here when I come in on Saturday," she remarked as Joey paused to shelve a book beside her.

"I like working Saturdays," the young woman said. "There are people who can't come in any other day, and I like seeing them."

Elena smiled at her. "And I like seeing someone who so loves their work."

"I do," Joey said with a smile.

"I believe my son attended one of your readings a few weeks ago. He came home raving."

Joey's smile widened. "He did! I remember he seemed quite entranced with the dragon in the story." She looked thoughtful. "You know, I believe a copy of that book came back in this morning. It's usually in high demand, but there's no hold on it at the moment. Do you think he might like to read it for himself?"

"I am willing to hope that he would. I would love to see him with an actual book in his hands again."

Joey's smile became a grin. "Ah! I thought I recognized a fellow purist! I love my e-reader, mind you, but sometimes only a paper book will do. Despite what Sean says," she added.

Elena told herself she was imagining the speculative gleam in the woman's green eyes. "I'm not surprised he's an electronic devotee," she said in a very neutral tone.

Joey nodded in agreement. "I'm not complaining, mind you. He helps us out a lot with our computer network. We haven't had to hire an IT person, which we can't afford, because of him."

"I did not know this." But somehow, she was not surprised. It clearly was in his nature to help where he could.

Joey nodded. "I swear, sometimes I think this town would fall apart without the Highwaters. So I'll forgive him the e-books. At least he reads. A lot."

"Does he?" This, she did not know either.

"Voraciously, Slater says. And that his retention is almost frightening. And coming from Slater, that's almost frightening," Joey added with another grin.

Elena laughed. "It is good to see you both so very happy."

"We are," Joey said. "Me, especially."

"I suspect he feels he is the lucky one."

Two spots of color rose in the woman's cheeks. "He does."

"That is the secret," Elena said, for some reason feeling even older than her years at the moment. "If you can keep that, you can conquer anything."

Joey smiled again, gave Elena another speculative look, glanced around as if to see if anyone was around, then said quickly, "Look, Elena, tell me to butt out if you want, but last night, there seemed to be…something, between you and

Sean."

"Something?" Elena said carefully.

"He doesn't usually get that edgy when he's working, but he sure did when you came up. I mean, I know he thinks you're like the Queen of Last Stand—"

"What?" Elena said rather sharply, completely startled.

"I...Slater told me he's always thought that. Like you and your family would be the royalty of Last Stand, if America went in for that."

"Which, thankfully, it does not," she said briskly.

But her mind was reeling a bit. Sean thought of her...like that? And always had? Her mother had always teased her that she carried herself like a queen, but she'd thought there had been pride beneath the teasing. She'd never thought that she might be keeping people at arm's length with it.

"I'm sorry if I—" She held up a hand and Joey stopped.

"You did not offend me, if that's what you're worried about. I was just...surprised. That he—that anyone would think of me that way."

"Slater says you can always tell how strongly Sean feels about something or someone by how edgy he gets."

Elena pondered this as she and Marcos—who was delighted to have the dragon book in hand—left the library. That Sean Highwater—any Highwater, she amended, as if that somehow took a little of the too-close feeling from it—would be...intimidated, or ill at ease with her for such a reason seemed unlikely, but she couldn't deny how often he seemed edgy whenever they were together.

Although dinner the other night had seemed relaxed enough. She felt a sudden tightness in her throat as she remembered how easily, how naturally he had picked up her sleeping son and carried him gently to the car. She didn't even have a name for the emotion that had welled up inside her then, unstoppable, until it had spilled down her cheeks in the form of tears. Tears he had stared at, but hadn't asked about, a forbearance she had been very grateful for. Because she did not think she could have explained the tangle of emotions, even to herself. She had no name for what she'd been feeling. She didn't know anything about what she'd been feeling.

Except it made you kiss him.

She shook off the shiver the memory brought, and told herself she should be thankful she'd managed to keep it to a kiss on the cheek. Her self-lecture did not help, for all it did was make her yearn to find out exactly what it would feel like, the kind of kiss she'd really wanted that night.

She gave herself a sharp, inward shake and focused on getting them safely home. The Saturday morning traffic normally wasn't a problem, but today, with the Christmas market, it was heavy enough that she wished to avoid it. She had just decided to make a loop to get back to the house from the other side when Marcos yelped.

"Stop, Mom!"

She hit the brakes simultaneously with a split-second glance in the mirror to be sure they weren't about to be rear-ended. Then she searched for something she'd missed, some car coming at them from somewhere, some animal she hadn't seen dart into the road.

"It's Sean, over by that stall with the cowboy boots!"

She breathed again. But somehow the juxtaposition, of Sean's name and the slamming on the brakes and bark of tires brought that long-ago day back to her in a rush. She'd heard the screech of the brakes that day at the restaurant, and the screams and shouts, that someone had been hit. She'd rushed outside, seen the group clustered around the still figure of a man in the street, their faces shocked and wide-eyed.

The last person in the world she would have expected it to be was Steven Highwater, the police chief of Last Stand. She had never hesitated to go to him, to try to help him, although the moment she looked into his Highwater blue eyes she'd known, and knew that he knew, too. He'd managed to get out a few words, even as he lay dying, absolving the distraught George Goetz of any blame, although the rest was cut short.

Not his fault…find him…my kids…tell them…

He'd been gone before he could give her whatever last words he'd wanted passed on to his children.

"—show him my book. Joey said he's read it."

She snapped back to the present. And her son's eagerness to share something special to him, such a rarity, broke down whatever resistance she had. She shook off the lingering chill of the memory and began to hunt for a place to park. She found a spot where a car with New Mexico plates was pulling out, and took it. Marcos was out of the car and hurrying back toward the marketplace, toward the rows of temporary stalls and kiosks stationed up and down Main Street and spilling over onto the side streets.

"No running in this crowd," she cautioned him. He didn't run, but he was still moving fast, and she had a moment to be glad she had worn comfortable shoes as she jogged after him, careful to keep him in sight.

He was far enough ahead of her that she had the chance to watch. He broke and ran the last few feet. Sean looked up the instant he did, and she saw him smile. It was a real, genuine smile. He was truly glad to see Marcos. And that did crazy things to her insides. As did the way, in the next moment, he looked around, searching the crowd.

For her. And she wasn't sure at this point if he was hoping to find her or not.

He leaned over to Marcos and said something, and her son gestured back the way they had come. She braced herself, and as she'd known he would, he looked that way and spotted her immediately.

He smiled again, but this time it was more hesitant. Almost shy.

...he thinks you're like the Queen of Last Stand.

Joey's words had seemed impossible in the library, but here, seeing firsthand the way he was looking at her, she couldn't deny they fit his expression.

A ridiculous scenario popped into her mind, born no doubt of too many romantic movies and stories. The commoner hopelessly in love with royalty, and unable to do anything about it because he was so beneath her, and she was untouchable to him.

And suddenly she was seized with a determination to show him just how wrong he was. At least, when it came to him.

She was not royalty. She was not untouchable.

Not to him.

Chapter Eighteen

"IT'S A GREAT story," Sean told Marcos. "I'll bet you read it all in one night."

Marcos looked slightly crestfallen. "Nah. My mom won't let me stay up all night."

"I think," she said, laying a hand on her son's hair, "that for reading a physical book I might make an exception."

She looked up from Marcos's startled but delighted expression to find Sean smiling at her. And in that moment at least, there was no hesitation, embarrassment, or distance between them.

"Whatcha looking for?" Marcos asked him, looking around at all the booths.

Sean blinked, as if he'd forgotten where he was. Or had mentally been somewhere else. Elena dared to hope it was the same place her mind had gone, to exploring whatever this was that sprang to life whenever they were together. Although perhaps she should instead simply hope that he felt it too, that it wasn't just some one-sided silliness from a…what? Prowling cougar? Love-starved widow? *Oh, think of some more clichés, Elena!*

"Christmas stuff," Sean said to Marcos. "Presents."

"You don't sound very happy about it," Elena said, brought out of her inane musings by his grimace.

"All of sudden I have…women to buy for."

"Ew," Marcos said with feeling.

"Plural?" Elena said, feeling a knot in her stomach. "More than…your sister?"

He nodded. "Lily and Joey now."

"You'll be buying gifts for your brother's girlfriends?"

He gave her a one-shouldered shrug. "Once they've done Sunday night at the ranch, they're family."

"What are you gonna get?" Marcos asked, giving her a moment to process what Sean had said.

"I have no idea. Sage is easy, all she ever wants is something for the ranch or her horses, but…Lily and Joey, they're more…"

"Girly?" Elena suggested rather archly when he stopped awkwardly.

"Yeah," he said, looking sheepish now. She found it, like so much else about this man, charming.

"Mom can help," Marcos offered helpfully. "She's real girly."

"I noticed," Sean said, and his voice had taken on the faintest of rough edges, some undertone that made her feel as if a finger had just run down her spine.

"She likes Christmas, too," Marcos added in a tone of warning. "Be careful or she'll make you start singing that silly 'Feliz Navidad' song."

"Believe me," Sean said solemnly, "nobody who's ever heard me sing would want that."

Your speaking voice is quite beautiful enough, Elena thought, then gasped when she realized she'd actually said it out loud. Sean practically gaped at her, and she would have sworn he flushed in the moment before he looked away from her. She felt heat rise in her own cheeks.

"My brother Kane had the singing voice," he muttered, and she knew how badly she'd embarrassed both of them, to make him bring up the Highwater who was never spoken of.

But there was such sadness in his voice that even in her embarrassment she couldn't stop herself from reaching out, putting a hand on his arm. "I pray that someday you find him, and that he is well."

He looked up then. "We have a newer lead, thanks to Slater and Joey."

"You do?"

He nodded. "A license plate and a vehicle description from a couple of years after he left. Nothing's turned up on it yet, but it's more than we had before."

"And you will never stop looking, will you."

"Never." He drew in a deep, audible breath. "We all feel...responsible, I guess. Because Kane said he always felt like the odd one out. I could relate to that feeling, being...odd. But I didn't see why he felt that way. As a kid I thought maybe it was because he was the only one whose name didn't start with an S. Or because he had different-colored eyes."

"That was...noticeable," she agreed. They were moving now, walking, and Elena realized it was because Marcos, bored by the adult talk, had started to wander around looking at all the offerings. And Sean had instinctively moved with him, keeping him in sight. Just as she would have done, had he not already. "But you believe differently now?" she asked.

"I think there was more to it. It took me a while to remember, but it was something he said when we were kids, working on a puzzle. That just because a piece fits in a place doesn't mean it belongs there."

She stopped moving. Felt an odd sort of pressure as she looked at him. "I believe that is one of the saddest things I've ever heard."

Sean nodded, looking oddly relieved. "You get it. Sage thought I was reading too much into it."

"It sounds…lost."

He was staring at her now. "That's how I felt, when he said it. He was only twelve then, but…he sounded so tired."

Which was, she thought, a very perceptive thing for a boy just two years older to have picked up on. But then, she'd never doubted he was perceptive. In fact, she guessed he was probably more so than most simply because he was more aware of other people than many were, for his own reasons.

Marcos came running back, asking if he could have a funnel cake. "I suppose," she said.

And before she could reach into her purse Sean had pulled out some folded cash and peeled off a bill. "Buy three," he said. "I'm starving."

"We'll wait on the bench," she called out as the boy ran for the stand that was sending out such luscious smells. They went and sat where they could see her son. But Elena's main focus was still Sean, and what they'd been talking about. She hesitated, then said it. "Your brother had already vanished by the time I got out there."

"I know." She saw his jaw tighten. "And I know what people think about what happened."

"Some people. The kind who always assume the worst about everyone. Which to me says much more about them."

"Yeah." He seemed to relax a little. And he gave her a smile that told her he appreciated her words.

"From what I recall of your father, he would say the same thing. Even about this."

"He believed intent counted. And he would never believe Kane intended what happened. He knew awful things could happen when people react out of emotion."

"Love?"

"And anger. Kane was angry a lot."

"What would he have been so angry about? Feeling as if he didn't belong?"

"Or worse," Sean said, rather flatly.

Marcos was there then, with the three fried treats. She took two of the sweet confections from her son, handed one to Sean, and gestured to Marcos to sit beside them. She said nothing, merely tore off a chunk of the fried, powdered-sugar-coated dough and popped it into her mouth. She rarely allowed herself such decadence, and savored it slowly. Then she licked the sugar from her thumb and forefinger.

Sean made an odd, choked sort of sound. She looked, saw him staring at her, and arched a brow at him. "Are you more of a rip it off with your teeth sort?" She nodded toward Marcos, who was working on his own funnel cake in that very rip it off with your teeth method she'd mentioned.

He swallowed visibly, although he didn't seem to have taken a bite. "I…used to be. When I was his age. Until I got tired of wearing more powdered sugar than I was eating."

One corner of her mouth curved upward as she glanced at her son, whose shirt now proved Sean's words. "I'll take hope from that, then."

He gave her a rather odd look, then started on his own funnel cake. She got through half of hers before she reached saturation with the sweetness and stopped. By then the strolling carolers had arrived, and were making the rounds. She saw Sean grimace.

"Don't care for Christmas carols?"

"No, they're fine. I think I'm just still mentally dealing with Thanksgiving."

She smiled. "The switch is a bit rapid when it's so late in the month."

He smiled at her. "Exactly. I'm not a big fan of floating holidays."

She studied him for a moment. "Prefer the predictability?"

He drew back slightly, but he was smiling. "Yes. Moving holidays disrupt the pattern."

"No wonder you and my son get along."

They listened to the singers—who truly were quite good—but as she did, she thought about what he'd said about his missing brother, and wondered what he'd meant by him feeling worse than just not belonging. And realized that she cared, a great deal, about this nagging unfinished business, if only because it bothered him.

She helped him pick out gifts, a book of human interest essays for Lily, who had begun writing similar articles for *The Defender*, and a beautiful hand-tooled, leather-bound journal for Joey. He'd watched with apparent interest as she'd tried a sample of the paper with her own fountain pen because she knew Joey used one to journal, saying he didn't realize the paper made a difference with fountain pens.

They were walking back toward her parked car when something struck her about what nagged at him. That perhaps an assumption she had always made about that day twelve years ago had been wrong.

"Marcos, go ahead and get into the car. I need to speak with Sean for a moment."

"You've been talking to him all afternoon," the boy pointed out, but got in willingly enough, probably because he had a full stomach and his book to read.

Sean was looking at her curiously now. "We *have* been talking all afternoon," he said in agreement with her son. Then, with that touch of shyness she found so endearing he added, "Sometimes about stuff I never, ever talk about."

"I know," she said softly. *And I am honored.* "And that is, in a way, what I wanted to tell you." She took a deep breath. "I presume you read…all the reports about that day."

His brow furrowed. "Yes." He grimaced. "Repeatedly."

She tried to think of a gentle way to put this. "I don't know exactly what they said about…what I told them.

About what your father said."

The furrows deepened. "They had what you said he told you, that it wasn't George's fault, and to find us and tell us…something. But he died before he could finish what he wanted you to tell us."

She took in a steadying breath. "Did they quote the exact words?"

"I don't know if it was exact. Why?" He was looking tense now. She couldn't blame him.

"Because I'm wondering now if we all misinterpreted what he said. His exact words were, 'Not his fault…find him…my kids…tell them…'"

He was staring at her. "Exact words?"

"They are engraved on my memory." She put a hand on his arm again. "It was the worst experience of my life to that point, and yet…I was glad I was there."

"I've always been glad you were there. And that you stayed with him to the end." He was staring down at her hand, but did not pull away. "That he wasn't alone."

His voice was low and tight, and she felt a tightness in her own throat. She hastened to finish while she could still speak. "I've always assumed the same as you have. But what if he wasn't absolving Mr. Goetz, didn't misspeak and say 'him' when he meant all of you, and what if he did say what he meant me to tell you?"

"Meaning?" There was a definite edge in his voice now.

She bit her lip, but at his rather fierce expression knew she couldn't back out of what she'd started now.

"What if instead of 'It wasn't George's fault, find my

kids and tell them,' he meant… 'It wasn't Kane's fault. Tell my kids to find him.'"

He went impossibly still. Stared at her. Said nothing.

"This fits much better with what I knew of him," she said, wondering if she should have kept it to herself.

"Yes," he said, almost hoarsely. And then, before she was even aware he was moving, he had pulled her into his arms, enveloping her in a fierce hug. "Yes, it does."

She felt a rush of relief. She tilted her head back to look at him about to say how grateful she was that she hadn't caused more pain, hadn't hurt him by bringing it up. She would never—

He kissed her.

And blasted all rational thought right out of her head.

Chapter Nineteen

SEAN HAD LEARNED the hard way over the years to resist many of his impulses. But there had been no resisting this one. Reckless though it might be, the memory of his father dying in the street had crazily sent his brain careening down the path of things he would regret if he dropped dead here and now, and at this instant in time not kissing her was at the top of the list.

Hell, right now it was the only thing on the list.

He'd figured it would feel good. That it would be hot. Even that it might spin him off into some kind of fantasyland where the peon really could capture the heart of the queen.

But that, and all other thought, was incinerated in the first instant. This wasn't just good, or hot, or a fantasy.

This was conflagration.

Her lips were soft, warm, and sweeter than his apparently feeble imagination could conjure up. He felt the kick of his pulse, a surge of sensation along every nerve, so fierce it threatened to swamp him.

And then, incredibly, she was no longer just allowing it but was kissing him back. Her lips parted, and he could taste even more of that impossible sweetness. And then he felt her tongue brush across his lips. He felt a leap in his chest, heard his heartbeat hammering in his ears, and if he'd turned to ash right here he wouldn't have been surprised. He wasn't sure he'd even regret it, because this would be one fine moment to die on.

He had no idea how long the sound had been going on before he noticed. Applause. They were being applauded. He jerked back. And the full realization of what he'd just done, kissed the woman who had been his dream for over a decade, in public, right next to the Christmas market, one of Last Stand's most popular events of the year, hit him. He didn't even look around, didn't want to know who was involved and have to face them later.

He didn't want to look at them anyway. He didn't want to look away from Elena. Even though he had no idea what to do, less idea what to say. Finally, he managed the only thing he could think of, although it came out in a whisper. "Those cakes weren't sweet enough."

Elena's eyes widened. He was surprised he even remembered how to breathe, the way she was looking at him. As if…as if…she were as stunned and breathless as he was.

"An early Merry Christmas, you two!"

That voice from behind him was familiar, and snapped him out of the pleasurable haze. He shot a glance over his shoulder, confirmed both that it had been Mark Latham, Shane's aide, and that he thankfully hadn't stopped to gape. Although the comment had sounded like a genuine good wish rather than teasing.

He looked back at Elena. "I'm sor—"

He stopped, his breath jamming up in his throat as she put one slender finger up to his lips. "Do not apologize. Not for that."

She whispered it, and belatedly he realized Marcos was right there. And suddenly staring at them, making Sean realize he'd seen that impossible, soaring, pulse-pounding kiss. And he wondered what Elena would say or do.

She said nothing more. What she did was simply open the driver's door and get in. "Thank you," she said as she reached for the handle. It took him a moment to realize she meant for the food. She did mean that, didn't she?

"Thank you," he said, but he meant it for the kiss. Then, recklessly, he decided to make that clear. "And for the help shopping, too."

He saw it register. Saw color rise in her cheeks. And the slight smile she gave him then seemed like a very private one, shared between two people who had more than one secret between them.

And then they were leaving, and Sean stood there for a long time after her car had vanished.

"YOU KISSED SEAN," Marcos said flatly.

It was more him kissing me, but I'm not going to quibble.

Nor would she deny what the boy had obviously seen. "Yes. Does that bother you?"

He grimaced. "When grown-ups like each other, they

kiss. I'm not stupid, Mom."

"Yes, sometimes they do. And I do like Sean."

"So do I," Marcos said, looking more thoughtful now. "Are you going to kiss him again?"

I can but hope. "How would you feel if I did?"

He gave her a sideways look. "Better'n when you kissed that Palmer guy."

She nearly laughed. "That you can blame on your cousin Esteban—he arranged that encounter."

Marcos wrinkled his nose. "Gran said that he doesn't choose the best friends sometimes."

"I can't argue that."

"She also said he's pretty," Marcos added with a laugh.

And neither she nor any of Esteban's multitude of girlfriends would argue that, either. The owner of Valencia's was, in fact, her cousin, making him a cousin once removed from Marcos, but the intricacies of that were of no interest to the boy so she hadn't pushed.

But right now she was glad the subject seemed to have been changed. And it lasted until dinner, when Marcos had blithely announced over his dessert that she and Sean had kissed.

Her mother did not even blink. She said serenely. "I'm glad to hear it."

Elena went still. "What?"

Her mother gave her a look that was as serene as her voice had been. "He is a fine, honest, respectful young man from an upstanding family, just the sort a mother would like to see her daughter with."

"I…see," Elena said.

"Not to mention," her mother said, with a glint in her eyes that Elena had not seen for a very long time, "that he is also handsome and very, very…" She glanced at Marcos and quite obviously changed what she'd been going to say. "Attractive," she finished.

And Elena knew perfectly well her mother, who could be as incorrigible as Marcos on occasion, had been about to say "sexy." An assessment she could hardly argue with, not after the way she had nearly burst into flame at one simple, short kiss.

"It has been a long time, Elena. Long enough. You have mourned him respectfully, and with love."

"Are you talkin' about my dad?" Marcos asked.

Elena decided she would let her mother get herself out of this one and silently went back to her meal. Being her mother, she didn't quail but approached it directly.

"I am speaking of both he and your mother. She loved your father very much, and he loved her just as much, but he is gone. I am saying he would want her—and you—to be happy. To have a full life, even if it is without him. To have the kind of life he died to protect."

"I wish he hadn't," Marcos said, in a voice so small Elena's chest contracted painfully.

"So do I," she whispered.

"But he did," her mother said firmly. "And we must accept it. And," she added with a pointed look at Elena, "move on. As he would have wished."

Later, after her mother had retired to her suite to read—

and watch her secretly beloved telenovelas, Elena suspected—and the warning timer Sean had set for her went off on Marcos's beloved game, instead of protesting he shut it down and turned to look at her.

"Would my dad have liked Sean?"

She went very still. This was a very significant question, and she must choose her words carefully.

"He did like him, Marcos."

Her son's eyes widened. "I didn't know they knew each other."

"They did not know each other well, but your father was friendly with both Sean and Chief Shane. He admired what they did, and once said their work was just as important as his."

"Oh." The boy said no more, but Elena didn't miss the thoughtful smile that curved his mouth.

And it wasn't until later, as she sat alone with the game console turned back on for something she would never admit, that she liked the music from the game, that another thought surfaced. Her immediate reaction to her son's question had been that it was significant. Very significant, and needing a serious, careful answer. Far more careful than if Sean was merely a friend, or someone she owed thanks to for helping Marcos.

Somewhere, in some part of her mind or heart, he had already become much more than that.

Chapter Twenty

SEAN PULLED OFF his shirt and inspected his arm, then flexed his left elbow experimentally. And grinned. Marcos had learned that last lesson well; he'd caught him off guard and put him on the mat with that leg sweep. And the kid had been deliriously happy about it. As he should be, given this was only his fourth lesson.

"I didn't hurt you did I?" Marcos sounded anxious now.

"Nah," Sean assured him. "But if we'd been out on a sidewalk somewhere, I'd be whining like a baby."

"You'd never whine," Marcos said with such confidence Sean felt a little humbled. Not knowing what to say to that he just grinned and took a swipe at the boy with his T-shirt. Then he gestured toward the tossed shoes and socks in the corner of the room.

"Gather up your stuff. Your mom'll be here soon."

"She already is," Marcos said, gesturing in turn toward the doorway out into the hallway.

Sean froze. Then, slowly, he turned around. And there she was, her hand still on the door handle, staring at him. With an expression that made him conscious of his bare chest and belly in a way he never was in this room where it wasn't at all unusual. He resisted the urge to check and see if his sweatpants had slipped a little too low, and instead just hoped they were heavy enough to mask his instant reaction to her.

"Get moving, then," he said, pleased his voice sounded almost normal. "Don't keep her waiting."

The boy scampered off to gather his clothes and school bag. Sean hastily pulled his shirt back on. Walked toward her, wondering if he should apologize for his state of undress. Decided not; it was a gym room after all.

"He's doing great," he said as he stopped in front of her. "Put me on the floor today."

"Is that why you were looking at your arm as if you needed to know if it still worked?"

She sounded concerned, so he smiled at her. "Just making sure." He glanced over to where Marcos was trying to stuff his shoes into the already full backpack. "And I was thinking. Wednesday will be a week since we started this, so a break might be good for him. Maybe he could come out to the ranch instead, if you don't mind. I'll bring him home after."

"I should be asking you if you mind."

"If I did I wouldn't have asked. He can hang out and see what it's like. If you think he'd like to."

"I know he would. He's been asking questions about life on a ranch that I'm afraid I have no answers to." She smiled. "My education and experience have been sadly lacking in that area, it seems."

Sean felt as if a door had just swung open in front of

him, and that with no idea where it would lead he had to decide in this instant whether to step through. And in that instant, he went with his heart and gut over his brain and that little warning voice.

"Broaden your horizons, then. Come with him."

He'd half expected her to look startled. She did not. Instead she gave him a smile that his heart and gut wanted to interpret as meaning she'd been hoping he'd ask.

"I would like that. Very much. The only time I get to see a horse up close is for the rodeo parade, and that doesn't seem right when I like them so much."

Sean swallowed past the lump in his throat. "We could ride. We've got a couple of really sweet, gentle horses you and Marcos could use."

"I believe I've ridden one of them a couple of times, for the parade."

"Whiskers. Of course," he said, feeling stupid for forgetting they loaned him out when a calm, gentle horse was necessary. But when he saw her—from a distance since he could never decide if he was going to look until the last moment—in that beautiful Mexican regalia draped over the saddle he barely even noticed the horse. Which, for a ranch-raised guy, was saying something.

"He seems quite sweet-natured."

"He is."

Marcos skidded to a halt beside them. "Who's what?"

"Whiskers is sweet," his mother said.

The boy blinked, then frowned. "That doesn't make sense."

"It does if you know Whiskers is a horse," Sean explained.

"Oh!" And then he looked from his mother to Sean. "Horse? Does this mean I get to go to your ranch?"

Sean felt more at ease now, and gave Elena a crooked smile. "He's quick, this one."

She smiled back. "Yes. He is. And sweet like Whiskers, too, when he wishes to be."

Marcos groaned. Sean laughed, knowing too well the last thing an eleven-year-old boy wanted to be known as was sweet.

"So, how about Wednesday afternoon, after school?" he asked. "I've got some time off coming."

"Can I, Mom? Please?"

"I will pick him up from school and bring him," she said. "Rosalina can handle anything that comes up at the restaurant, or call me if she cannot."

So. She would come. Now he just had to see that she stayed after they arrived. Because he wanted her to see the place, to see how he lived, and to see how she reacted.

And why that was so important to him he wasn't sure he wanted to face.

ELENA SLOWED AS they neared the turn. The intricate stonework fence and pillars were solid and beautiful. The arched metal gate with the circled Lone Star in the center was simple but evocative. And the Lone Star flag at full mast on the pole to the right of the gate rippled in the breeze. The house wasn't visible from here, and the entrance road curved and disappeared through a thick stand of trees. She knew the Highwater ranch was smaller than it once had been, that they'd had to sell off some acreage back during a bad patch, but it was still more land than she could imagine keeping up with.

There was also a freestanding pillar, shorter, along the left side of the entrance, which housed an intercom. She realized she would have to announce their arrival to get in, and wondered who would be on the other end. She pulled to a stop beside the device, rolled down the window and reached out.

"Wait, Mom! I have a code."

She looked at the number pad. "A pass code?"

"Yeah. Sean told me what to do," he said excitedly. She thought about just making him tell her the number, but he was so excited she couldn't do it. He'd been anticipating this afternoon all day today, and most of yesterday.

"How fast can you get out, run over and punch it in, and get back in the car?"

"Before the gate opens all the way," he promised.

Moments later he proved himself right, the passenger door slamming shut before the gate slipped completely clear of the road. She drove through the opening, toward the stand of trees fifty yards ahead, trying to picture them in spring when they would be fully leafed out. It would be a wide swath of green, she could tell. And lovely.

The road dipped, then rose again, then repeated, giving

her the sense of truly being in the Hill Country, more than she ever felt in town. And she was surprised at how much it tugged at something inside her, something deep and basic. She needed to get out here more.

Well, not specifically to the Highwater Ranch of course, but out where she could see and sense the hills that had given this home she loved its name. There were benefits to living in town, the closeness to the restaurant, and to all the amenities, but this, this called to her. Besides, the house was still her mother's, and while she had made them more than welcome and insisted she loved having them there, Elena still felt a bit hemmed in by living in the house she'd grown up in. She'd gotten used to being in charge, especially when Enrique had been deployed, and it had been difficult to cede control of the household.

Perhaps that was why she had been so stern with Marcos in the beginning. Not only because she was terrified of losing him as she had his father, but also because he was the only thing she was fully in charge of, back when he'd been a rambunctious six-year-old.

But he was growing so fast now, and in less than two years he would be thirteen. And she felt another tug deep inside at the thought of being the single mother of a teenager.

"There's the house!" Marcos yelped. "Wow, it's big."

"It must be, since all the Highwaters live there."

"And is that a…a barn? Where horses live?"

"I believe it is," she said with a smile.

"And look, somebody's riding!"

She looked where he was excitedly pointing, toward a fenced enclosure surely too large to be called a corral, although she had no idea what it would be called. But there was definitely a horse, a sleek, golden brown animal who seemed to be flowing rather than galloping in a big circle.

And aboard him was Sean. She slowed to a halt.

"Why are you stopping?" Marcos protested.

"I want to watch for a moment."

Apparently that was acceptable, because he said, "Okay."

She knew just enough about balance and riding to stay in the saddle during the slow walk down Main Street during the rodeo parade. This was an entirely different matter. This was skill, power and grace, a melding of horse and rider that was on a level far above anything she'd ever aspired to. He might not be the rodeo rider his brother Shane was, but obviously Sean was quite at home on a horse.

Only then did she notice the other person there, a young woman who had been sitting on the top rail of the fence, but now swung over and dropped down outside the fence. And headed toward them.

"Who's that?"

"That is Sean's sister, Sage," Elena said, recognizing her both from her frequent stops at the restaurant and her blazing demonstrations of reining and cutting horses at the rodeo.

Marcos's eyes widened. "She looks like a cowgirl."

"Indeed she does," Elena said, watching the tall, slender woman, with long, dark hair in a single thick braid down her back approach. She was dressed in a long-sleeved blue shirt, jeans, and a pair of well-worn chaps, the style Elena thought was called shotgun. Her expression was not particularly welcoming, and Elena's brow furrowed.

"You can park over there," Sage said, gesturing toward a space out of the way toward the house. Her tone matched her expression.

Marcos barely waited until the car had come to a stop before leaping out. He looked up at Sage. "Sean says you're the toughest cowgirl in Texas."

And that easily her entire demeanor changed. She looked at the boy and smiled, and it was a warm, genuine one. "Does he, now? I'm glad to see that lesson finally got through to him."

"He says you can outdo most cowboys, too."

"Well, now you've done it." Her smile at Marcos became a grin. "Now I'm going to have to make him cookies."

"Can I go watch him?" the boy asked, looking eagerly toward man and horse.

"You can sit on the fence. Just don't go in the arena," Sage cautioned. "Poke's working."

Marcos nodded and took off at a run. And the moment her son was gone, Sage shifted back to an expression that was almost unreadable, but certainly not the bright welcome she'd given Marcos. She didn't think she'd ever done anything to antagonize the young woman. In fact their encounters at the restaurant and elsewhere in town had been pleasant, so she was not certain what was wrong.

Sage matched her own five foot eight, so she met her gaze levelly. "You are not happy to see me here."

Sage's eyes, which were yet a different Highwater blue, almost the color of the bluebonnets that blanketed the Hill Country in the spring, widened slightly. "Well, that was direct."

"You've always impressed me as a direct sort of woman."

Sage's mouth curved the tiniest bit as she nodded. "Sean's told me enough about Marcos to know that he's made a strong connection with your son."

"He has. And he has helped me tremendously to understand Marcos, how he thinks, why he reacts the way he does sometimes."

"Or doesn't react?" Sage suggested.

"Exactly that," Elena agreed, smiling at just how much help Sean had given her.

"Sean hasn't always had the easiest time, and I'm guessing you understand from Marcos why. They think differently, and some people aren't very understanding or forgiving of that."

"That is, sadly, quite true. And Sean has been a great help to Marcos in handling that. But just what is it that's bothering you?"

Sage seemed to hesitate. "I hope you've made it clear to him that that's all you want. Help with your son."

Elena went very still. Stared at the young woman, whose expression had become almost mutinous now. Elena said nothing, because in that moment she could find no words.

"Look," Sage said after a moment, "Sean would hate me telling you this, but he's had this weird thing about you for years. Been kind of in awe."

What Joey Douglas had told her came back in a rush: *...he thinks you're like the Queen of Last Stand.*

"I have never wished for this," she said carefully.

"That doesn't matter. What matters is that it gives you the power to really hurt him, and I don't want my brother hurt."

Elena studied the woman before her, saw the fiercely protective look in her eyes. Acknowledged it with a nod before saying, sincerely, "I admire and appreciate your love for your brother. But you're mistaken."

Sage looked startled. "I know my brother," she insisted.

"I meant," Elena said, "in thinking the only thing I want from him is help with my son."

And there it was, at last, in so many words, what she'd been dancing around for days now. And since there was not a single thing to say after that, she simply walked away, leaving Sean's sister staring after her.

Chapter Twenty-One

HE'D KNOWN THEY were here, he'd heard the chime of the system announcing someone had keyed in the gate code. Even focused on Poke and his workout, he'd heard the car, seen it out of the corner of his eye. If it wasn't for the fact that he'd agreed to work the horse so Sage could watch, see things in a way she couldn't when she was the one aboard, he would have stopped right then.

He didn't change or shift when he saw Marcos clamber up to the top rail, and neither did Poke. Sage had trained him so well he barely flicked an ear toward the fence as they went by. So Sean knew the horse was aware of the boy, but he wasn't about to let a new arrival distract him from the mission at hand, honing that reining skill to a high edge. The least he could do was go along, and focus on that mission himself.

And then he saw Elena.

Poke kept going because he was well trained, but Sean completely lost all awareness of what the hell he was supposed to be doing. Because as gorgeous as she was in her usual, more polished attire, Elena de la Cova was breath-stealing in form-fitting black jeans and a snug black sweater.

And the form they fit had his pulse hammering and his breath quickening.

In all those years he'd never quite realized, or allowed himself to realize, how...how utterly female she was. But it had never been about sexiness before, because he'd never dared even think about her like that. For years he'd had some pristine vision of her in his mind, as if she were some untouchable, beautiful sculpture far beyond his vision and reach.

That kiss had blasted that all to bits. Maybe that's why it seemed so different now. Why all he could see now was this living, breathing woman with the flashing eyes and luscious shape. Or maybe it was simply because she was here, on his home turf, the ranch. Was it as simple as seeing her where he'd never expected to? Or maybe it was a throwback, to all those times when, desperate for distraction, he'd tried to picture her here, in this place, in his life. He'd never been able to really pull that off—it was too distant from his reality. It hadn't been distant from his fantasy, though. He remembered one of the games he'd played endlessly in the days after his father's funeral. A game where the goal was to rescue the kidnapped princess, and you were allowed to choose the avatar for the endangered royal. He'd picked the dark-haired, dark-eyed beauty instantly, and was well into the game before he'd realized why. He'd—

"Hey, nerd-brain! Snap out of it."

Sage's shout yanked him back to the present. Poke had come to a halt in the middle of the arena, clearly puzzled by the sudden lack of presence of his rider. He felt himself flush;

it had been a long time since he'd lost himself while on a specific task that required focus. He'd dared to hope he'd broken the habit permanently, but obviously he had not.

He leaned over and gave Poke an apologetic pat on the neck. "Sorry, buddy. My fault."

Poke tossed his head and snorted, in a "Don't let it happen again," sort of way. Sean knew it wouldn't, because Sage might not ever let him ride her most prized animal again.

"Finish the pattern," Sage called out. "Or you'll really mess him up."

He doubted that. Poke was too smart and Sage had done too good a job training him, but when it came to this, his sister was the boss. Shane had made that clear the day they'd all voted to put the ranch and stock in her care.

So he sent the horse back into an easy lope, thinking he wouldn't mind a little more time to recover from his unexpected lapse before he actually had to face Elena. He knew since she was here by his invitation he should be there to welcome her, in fact should never have gone ahead with this ride in the first place, but Sage had asked and she rarely did, so—

He cut off his own thoughts before he spiraled off again, and focused on Poke. They'd been just over halfway through the reining pattern, having just completed the spins to the left. Poke had been solid throughout, his rollbacks powerful, that hind leg so planted on the spins so that you'd swear he was on a post.

Now he lifted the reins and cued the horse to start the rest of the pattern. Circles to the left, large and fast first, then smaller and slower, then the large and fast again. At the cue Poke executed a perfect flying change of leads and struck out to the right, repeating the circle pattern. And then they were on the last segment, a straight, fast run that culminated in a sliding stop that had Poke's hindquarters practically on the ground as his back hooves dug in, never wavering or hopping, sending up a spray of dirt behind them.

He heard a yelp from the fence. Marcos. He started to grin, feeling better. Those sliding stops were pretty flashy, and he suddenly was glad Marcos—and Elena—had been here to see it.

"Perfect," he told the horse, and reined him around to head for them.

"Not bad, your geekiness," Sage teased as he pulled the horse to a halt.

"It's almost like he was trained," he shot back. Sage laughed.

"Wow, that was cool!" Marcos was grinning widely, and sounded about ready to bubble over with excitement.

"Marcos, meet Poke. Short for Highwater's Hot Poco."

"That's a funny name."

"It comes from one of his ancestors, who was famous. And he's a really, really good horse. Sage is getting the most out of him."

Marcos gave Sage a shy but admiring look as she jumped down off the fence. He kicked free of the stirrups, swung a leg over Poke's neck and slid off. Sage was there, taking the reins, before he hit the ground.

"Thanks, Bro."

"You bet. Not sure what there is left to work on with him, though. He felt golden all the way, except for that moment of operator error."

She gave him a forgiving smile, then nodded. "Nothing left but to do it."

Sean grinned at her. "Oklahoma City, here you come."

"Don't jinx it," she said.

He gave her a hug; this was the only thing in life Sage was nervous about, her horses. But when she was in close, he heard her whisper, "Be careful, Sean. Be sure."

He pulled back to look at her, brow furrowed. She indicated Elena with a shift of her eyes. "Yeah," he muttered. "I got it. Don't be stupid."

"Impossible," Sage said, patting him on the back before she let go, turned, and swung up on Poke. She looked over at the two by the fence. "Y'all have fun, now. I'm going to take Poke to the creek. Slater was out early and said it's running full."

"He's getting downright ranch-handy, isn't he?" Sean quipped.

"Because Joey loves it out here. One more thing to thank her for. By the way, there's lasagna and garlic bread for everybody in the fridge."

And then his sister was gone, heading out to let the horse who loved splashing in water play a little after his workout. Leaving him a little stunned. His little sister was a paradox, warning him but fixing her signature meal for them. She who refused to be relegated to the kitchen just because she was "the girl."

He turned to finally face Elena. And suddenly he couldn't think of a thing to say, and doubted he could have gotten any words out if he could. Thankfully, she did it for him.

"What's in Oklahoma City?"

"Oh. The NRHA—that's the National Reining Horse Association," he explained, adding with a glance at Marcos, "as opposed to the NHRA, which is the National Hot Rod Association," which made the boy laugh. "Anyway, it's their annual competition, the derby, this June. She's going to take Poke and compete."

"I wish them both great luck," Elena said with a smile.

"I hope they do well," Sean said. "She'll feel bad if they don't. Not for herself, but she'll feel like she let Poke down."

"That says a lot about her."

"Family's first with her, and her horses are family."

"I can see that."

"I hope they win!" Marcos exclaimed.

"They could," he said, then added wryly, "as long as she's riding, and not nerd-brain here."

"Rabbit-hole moment?" Elena asked, but she was smiling.

"Afraid so." *And what would you think if you knew you were the one who sent me down that rabbit hole?*

"You recovered nicely."

"Poke did. He's that good. Best we've ever had."

"That stop thing was amazing," Marcos said.

"It was. Now, you ready to meet your horse for the day?"

The boy was practically dancing with excitement all the

way to the barn. He was so wound up he ran ahead, and stood peeking in the big sliding door. Leaving Sean alone with Elena. And again searching for something to say. Finally settled on what was, to him, an undeniable truth.

"You look wonderful. You should wear jeans more often." He heard his own words and nearly groaned aloud. He looked away, shaking his head in disgust. "Like I'm the one to decree what any woman should wear."

"And why not?"

He gave her a sideways glance. "Sage calls me a sartorial coward."

"Because you always wear black? I imagine some would say the same about me."

"But you look great in it."

"As do you. So why not?"

The memory of that kiss was suddenly alive and crackling between them, so powerfully he thought it must almost be visible. He was afraid of careening out of control, and grabbed desperately at his first thought. "I always thought you wore it because…" He trailed off, wishing he'd diverted this a while back.

"For Enrique?" He nodded. To his amazement she smiled. "Perhaps that is how it began, but as a working single mother, the less time I have to spend thinking of my wardrobe, the better."

"That makes sense."

"And you?"

He shrugged. "Started for the same reason, I think. My dad. Then it was just easier."

"So we are simply practical."

"Maybe just no reason to change. What difference would it make?"

"You looked rather festive in your red tie," she said.

"I like red," he admitted. "But that's about as far as my color scheme daring goes."

She laughed, and he felt that little burst of happiness inside that he always felt when he managed to make her smile or laugh. She was here, it wasn't an imagined fantasy, and he told himself to soak it in, to savor it, because it would likely never happen again.

The queen didn't make a habit of visiting the commoners.

Chapter Twenty-Two

ELENA COULDN'T DENY she felt a little nervous. For herself as well as for Marcos, who was so excited about his first time riding a horse that he was chattering. He never chattered, usually it was a chore to get him to actually talk. But he'd practically blossomed since Sean had come into their lives, and she would be ever grateful.

...that's all you want. Help with your son.

Sage's words came back to her, and she looked at him as he adjusted the stirrups on the saddle for Marcos, and gave him—and her, she supposed—instructions on how to handle the obviously very gentle animal. Did he believe that? Did he truly think that it was only his knack with her son that she valued? How could he, after...that kiss? Surely that made it clear that there was more than simple gratitude between them?

But if what Sage—and Joey—had said was right... He was not truly in awe of her, was he? How could he be, when he was a Highwater, and they had been in Last Stand as long as her own family had been? She must truly think about this, for the last thing she wanted was for him to feel she thought him somehow beneath her. If she was doing something, acting in ways that made him think this, it must stop, for that had never, ever been her intention. The last thing she wanted was to hold him off, at a distance. The opposite, in fact. She wanted to be closer to him. She wanted him to be closer to her.

She simply wanted him.

She felt a sudden flush of heat. It had been a very long time since she'd had such thoughts, and she had the feeling she was not handling them well. As a twenty-nine-year-old widow and single mother, she'd made some assumptions, and one of those was that there would be no one who could make her feel the way her husband had. She had thought that aspect of her life over, even as she regretted having to close it off at such a young age. But she was sure no one would ever make her want, in the way a woman wanted a man, again.

She'd been wrong.

With a great effort of will she forced her thoughts onto another path. Marcos, since those were the only thoughts that seemed powerful enough to pull her off of Sean. She wondered if Marcos felt something like Sage said Sean felt, around the more popular children at school, not simply as if he did not belong, but as if they were above him. She must ask him—

"It'll be fine, he is really calm, like Whiskers."

She blinked, and focused on Sean who had come to stand beside her and the black and white pinto horse she was on. Realized her expression must have seemed worried.

"I…I'm fine, really," she said. "I wasn't concerned. I believe I just fell down one of your rabbit holes."

He drew back, one corner of his mouth twitching in that way she was coming to quite like. "I didn't realize it was catching."

She smiled. Hesitated, then decided she'd better just say it. "I was just hoping you understood that while I greatly appreciate your help with—" she flicked a glance at her son, who was happily patting the neck of the docile sorrel horse called Whiskers "—things, I like even more…spending time with you. I like you a great deal, Sean Highwater."

He stared at her, and for a moment she thought she'd mistaken everything, that she'd been foolish in thinking—

"Elena."

It was barely above a whisper, and there was a hoarse, rough note in his voice that sent a shiver through her. And the heat that flared in the eyes she usually thought of as an ice-blue shade made them anything but icy.

"We goin' or not?" Marcos called out.

"Hold that thought," Sean said, still holding her gaze.

"With pleasure," she said, meaning it.

He turned on his heel then. She watched him stride over to the powerful-looking gray horse he'd saddled for himself, and swing into the saddle with the ease of long practice. She didn't doubt what he'd told her, that he'd once been as awkward as Marcos, but it was hard to believe looking at him now. He seemed the epitome of Texas cowboy grace and power.

And she dared to hope that someday her son would reach that same point, with his own particular kind of confidence.

If he did, she knew whatever happened between now and then, part of it would be due to the influence of Sean Highwater in his life.

"THIS VIEW IS wonderful," Elena said as they stopped the horses on the ledge overlooking the expanse of the hills rolling into the distance. He'd brought her here for this, because if the Hill Country was the place of your heart, this vista couldn't help but speak to you.

Even Marcos was impressed. Not as impressed as he was with Whiskers, but enough to say, "It's like you can see forever."

"It was always Dad's favorite spot to come and think," Sean said. "And Shane's now."

He watched her as she looked out over the rolling hills, saw her take a deep breath and let it out slowly, as if the peace of the place was stealing over her.

"I can see why. It is a reminder of why this land is special, different. Thank you for bringing me here."

"You should come back in the spring, when the bluebonnets are out. Those hills are covered as far as you can see, and at the right time of morning or evening, when the sky is that sort of purple-blue, you can't tell where the sky stops and they start."

"That was...lovely," she said softly, and the appreciation in her voice kept him from feeling embarrassed; he hadn't meant to blurt all that out. "And," she added with a sideways look that had him holding his breath, "if that was an invitation, I accept."

Spring. Months from now. Future plans. Plans to be together.

The words rocketed through his brain, leaving a trail of firing neurons in their wake. And all his inner warnings not to misinterpret couldn't even begin to be heard over the bedlam.

"It's a date," he said, his voice so tight he thought it a wonder the words even came out.

"I shall hold you to it."

"Can we ride some more?" Marcos asked, clearly oblivious to—or not caring about—the suddenly charged atmosphere. He did feel a kinship with the boy, and honestly hoped he was helping him, but right now he found himself wondering what would have happened if he wasn't here.

And the memory of that kiss exploded through him, making his voice so tight this time it cracked. "We—sure. Head down there."

He pointed out the trail to the west that led down to the creek. The boy was actually doing fairly well for someone who'd never been on a horse before. A little zealous with his heels and on the reins, but the ever-patient Whiskers tolerated children better than any horse he'd ever known.

He noticed Elena watching her son go. "Whiskers knows that trail, they'll be fine."

"I wasn't worried." She turned to look at him. "Not about them, anyway. I'm selfishly more concerned about myself. I love this, but it's not something I grew up doing."

"You'd never know it. You look like you belong on a horse. Different than the parade, there you always look…regal, but now you look pretty at ease."

It was a moment later, as they started after Marcos on the trail that was wide enough for them to ride side by side, that she spoke. Quietly, with a note of concern in her voice he'd not heard before.

"You said regal." He shrugged, avoiding her eyes, not sure what to say. "I have heard more than once—please do not ask me from whom—that you look at me this way."

I'm betting Sage for one, damn it. "I can guess," he muttered.

"Do you feel this way because you believe I think I am better than anyone else?"

Startled, his gaze shot to her face. "No!" Something in her dark, bright eyes warned him to tread honestly. "It's how you speak, so beautifully, and how you carry yourself, like someone who's rightfully proud of her family and history." He finished rather lamely, "It's just how I've always thought of you."

"As regal?"

"Yes." And then he did something he'd never, ever thought he would. He held her gaze and added, "Queen Elena."

She laughed, a sound tinged with disbelief. "Who manages a restaurant?"

"That has nothing to do with it."

She considered that for a moment. "I see." Yes, he was really coming to hate that phrase. "I do not think I like this."

His stomach knotted. "I mean it with the greatest respect."

"I realize this. But if I am a queen, that means there are subjects."

"Us peons?" he suggested, trying to lighten the mood he seemed to have unintentionally caused.

"Sean." He looked up when she stopped after his name. She studied him for a long, silent moment. "I have made you feel this way? Done something, said something?"

"No! It's me. It's just...how I've always felt."

"You believe I think you beneath me?"

"No!"

"Then you think it about yourself?"

"Maybe." He lowered his gaze, rubbed at an imaginary bit of dirt on the saddle horn.

"Is this why you never come into the restaurant? You've been avoiding it because of this?" His gaze shot back to her face. He hadn't expected her to make that jump. "I assumed it was because of what happened, that your father was killed in the street in front."

"It's not my favorite location."

"And of course a peon, so far beneath her, cannot just visit the queen."

She was making it—and him—sound ridiculous. And maybe he was. Maybe he always had been. Maybe inside he was still that geeky, weird kid who never quite related to the world in the way others did. In that moment it was as if it had all fallen away, all the growth he'd managed, everything he'd learned about how to at least appear more normal, and he was indeed that kid with the brain that worked in strange ways.

"Exactly," he said, unable to stop the sourness of his thoughts from echoing in his voice.

She glanced ahead, as if to see where Marcos was. And then she looked back at him. And when she spoke, her voice low and with a husky note that made every part of his body tighten, her words nearly blasted him out of the saddle.

"There is only one way I think of you beneath me, Sean Highwater. And there is nothing queenly about it."

Chapter Twenty-Three

ELENA COULDN'T QUITE believe she'd said it. For a usually reserved—regal?—woman, it seemed she was losing touch with all boundaries. At least, around this man she was.

And now she'd shocked him. He wasn't just staring at her, he was gaping at her. And why not, when she'd just made a beyond suggestive remark with her son barely out of earshot?

"If I have misjudged, I apologize. But for the first time in years I have been reminded that I am not just a mother, but still a living, breathing woman. And I thank you for that, even if I am wrong about...how you feel about me."

"No."

It broke from him as if the single syllable was all he could manage. As if she'd struck him nearly dumb. The question was, what exactly was he saying no to?

"No...to what?"

"Not wrong."

Only one more word, but it was enough. It answered what she most needed to know. "Then perhaps we should pick up this discussion again in a different setting? Or at least alone," she added as they reached the bottom of the slope where Marcos had stopped.

At that moment the boy looked at them. "You know what I really like about this place? There's no Mr. Strickland."

"Mr. Strickland?" Sean asked, sounding almost grateful for the distraction. As was she.

"Our neighbor next door," Elena explained. "He's a bit cranky and very protective of his garden."

"Oh. Yeah, you have to go a ways to get to the neighbors here. But it's the McBrides, so they're not cranky."

"The medical McBrides?" Elena asked; she knew both Doctor Turner McBride and Doctor Graham McBride from assorted town functions, and the paramedic they'd seen at the toy drive, Spencer, often stopped in at the restaurant for food to take back to the station. She'd been vaguely aware they lived on a place out here, but hadn't realized it was next to the Highwater ranch.

"I think their sister would protest that," Sean said. He looked at Marcos. "Jessie rescues mustangs."

The boy's eyes widened. "You mean wild horses?"

"Yes. She's got a half dozen or so over there now. Sage helps her out with them now and then."

"Could we go see 'em sometime?" Marcos asked excitedly.

Sean looked at her. Marcos sighed and grimaced. As if he expected her to of course say no. "If she would be willing," she said. Marcos's expression changed instantly into an excited grin.

"Maybe after the holidays. I'll check with her, see when would be good," Sean said.

Marcos was delighted. And when they dismounted to let the horses drink before starting back, the boy announced, "I want to be a detective when I grow up," and then promptly went to explore the creek for possible fish.

Elena felt a qualm at the idea of her son in a dangerous profession. Which reminded her the man she was rapidly falling for already was. As Enrique had been, and had ended up paying the ultimate price for his desire to serve.

Not wanting to think about it, she tried to reroute her thoughts. "Did you join the department because of your father and your brother?" she asked.

"This department, yes. I've been…approached by other, bigger cities. But I'd never transfer. Shane cuts me slack because he knows I think different."

"I believe your…what do they call it? Your clearance rate? I think that may have more to do with it."

He smiled at that. "Maybe. But really, I've known what I wanted since I was fourteen and my dad laid out a case for me. He told me all the evidence, the victims, the suspects, and asked me what I thought. It was like this big, complex puzzle, with the unpredictable human factor messing up the logic."

"That must have been a thrill for you, your father asking for your help."

"It was, at that moment. He told me later what he'd been trying to do was get me to understand people better. He didn't expect me to solve the case."

"But you did?"

"Well, it was already solved, actually. It was an old case. But I figured it out without knowing that."

"And the die was cast," she said with a smile.

"Yeah." His grin was almost boyish, and she felt as if she'd had a glimpse of that fourteen-year-old.

"It sounds like you had a wonderful relationship."

"We did. He was a great guy." His gaze shifted to look out into the distance. "Except he fell in love with the wrong woman."

"And yet look at the family that produced. That evens it out, in a way, doesn't it?"

He looked back at her then, and his voice was soft when he said, "Yes. Yes, it does."

It was later, when they had gone back to the house and Sean had the lasagna and garlic bread in the oven, that Marcos looked at her and said, with that bluntness she sometimes despaired of, "You've been a lot more fun since we started hanging out with Sean."

Out of the corner of her eye she saw Sean freeze in the act of getting plates from a cupboard. And she had the sudden feeling her answer to this could be important.

"I have been having a lot more fun," she said. "As have you. I believe I had forgotten how to, but he has reminded me."

"Cool," Marcos said blithely. Sean moved again.

"Put these on the table over there, will you, buddy?" Sean held the plates out to the boy.

"Sure," he said cheerfully, took them and trotted off to

the dining area.

Sean looked at her then. "That was quite a compliment."

"It was nothing less than the truth," she said.

For a moment he just looked at her, then, softly, he said, "Me, too."

What she had said out in the hills seemed to hover between them for a moment. But Marcos was still here, and this was not a conversation she wanted to have with him so near.

"May I ask you something?" she said instead.

"Anything." The way he said it proved he, too, had felt her words hanging in air suddenly fraught.

"Did you feel…guilty, the first time you laughed, or enjoyed something, after your father was killed?"

He looked startled, then thoughtful. "Yes. Like I had no right to laugh, to feel good or cheerful. Like it was betraying him somehow, to laugh about anything, when he was gone."

She nodded slowly as she let out a long breath. "I think that is why I resisted even the idea of enjoyment for so long. It felt…disrespectful somehow."

He moved then, coming over to her and taking her hands in his. "I only met him a couple of times, but I know he was crazy about you. And the kind of man he was would never want you to die with him. And," he added with a glance toward Marcos, "he'd be proud of you both."

There was nothing of the attraction between them in this. This was simply a good, honest man trying to comfort, and doing it by praising the absent man who was, in a way, a barrier between them.

"I have said it before, but it bears repeating. You are a kind and wise soul, Sean Highwater."

Silence spun out between them before Sean asked, sounding as if he were trying not to, "I know you do and will always love him. But are you still...in love with him?"

She drew in a deep breath as it sparked back to life, this thing between them. "No. That kind of love requires give and take from both sides. And he is not here to do that. He can only remind me of how sweet it can be."

"I've...never known how sweet it can be."

She held his gaze, that blue Highwater gaze, and tried to put what she was feeling into her voice. "Then perhaps, as you have taught me how to have fun again, I can...teach you."

And then Marcos was back, once more cutting short a conversation they needed to have. His easy chattering with Sean was too precious for her to truly mind. And it seemed a short time later they were at the table, she serving up slabs of the wonderful-smelling pasta dish while Sean dealt out slices of the equally luscious-smelling bread.

"Are you comin' for Mom's birthday?" Marcos asked after a few minutes, as he dug in for another bite of the lasagna that was clearly a hit with him.

"Marcos," Elena began, then stopped. Curiously, she asked, "Which do you mean?"

Marcos looked at Sean consideringly. Sean merely looked puzzled. "At the house," Marcos pronounced firmly. "On the real day."

The way he said it make Elena smile inwardly. That he

wanted Sean there, on the more personal, intimate day, warmed her.

"The 'real' day?" Sean asked.

"Our extended family will acknowledge my birthday at the feast day gathering at the restaurant on Thursday."

"The Virgin of Guadalupe?"

She smiled; somehow she'd known he would know. "Yes."

"But that's not your actual birthday?"

"No. It is just easier, since everyone is already together."

"Too many of them," Marcos said. "I don't think you'd like it so much. So come Saturday. Then it's just Mom and Gran and me."

Sean hesitated, looking at her. Then he said quietly, "Please don't feel you have to—"

"What I would feel," she said, "is honored, if you would join us."

"I'd like that," he said softly. "If your mother wouldn't mind."

"Mind? She quite likes you, Mr. Highwater."

"And I'm not nearly as afraid of her as I used to be."

"That's because you did not have her as a teacher," she teased.

He grinned at her. "My brothers would agree with that."

A new voice came from the doorway. "What am I agreeing to? Besides a big helping of lasagna, that is?"

Elena looked up to see the middle brother, Slater coming through the doorway. If he was surprised to see her here it didn't show. Marcos, unfamiliar with this Highwater, fell silent, and his easy smile faded. It tugged at her, this evidence that he still had that shell to retreat into when confronted with strangers.

"The fearsome reputation of Mrs. Valencia," Sean said.

Slater grinned. "I liked her. She knows her stuff." He looked at Elena. "Mrs. de la Cova." He said it with a polite nod, and she couldn't help noticing it was different than the respectful, rather awed dip of the head Sean had given her. Which in turn made her realize just how far they'd come from that, in a short time.

"Elena, please," she said. Slater smiled. It was odd, she thought. All the Highwater men were quite attractive, and Slater's eyes were the most amazing shade of turquoise blue, but she found she preferred Sean's light blue. She just preferred Sean, period.

"Hey, Bro," Slater said, "Joey wanted to know if you'll still be able to get in this Sunday while they're closed, to finish the network setup on the new computer lab."

"I'm planning on it," Sean said. "Where is she, anyway?"

"Out with Bella McBride, plotting mayhem I'm sure."

Sean grinned. "Good for them."

"Is that library Joey?" Marcos asked, casting Slater a very wary look, and asking the question of Sean.

"Yep," Sean said. Then he leaned over and said in a loud whisper, "For some reason she's crazy about my brother."

"Oh." When Marcos looked at Slater again, it was with a little less trepidation. "I like her."

"So do I," Slater said with a wink at the boy.

"You're going to set up a new computer lab at the library?" Marcos asked Sean.

He nodded. Then gave Elena a questioning look, and a half nod toward her son. She smiled, and nodded back.

"Maybe you'd like to come and help," Sean said to the boy.

Marcos stared at Sean, almost awed. "Yes!" he yelped. Then he looked at her. "Can I, Mom?"

"Since it is for the library, and will help Joey, yes, you may."

"Cool!" He looked back at Sean and said proudly, "I'm good with computers."

"I figured you were. Although it's kind of tricky, doing stuff other people will use."

Marcos frowned. "What do you mean?"

"I mean you can't assume everybody knows as much as you do. And you have to think about not just what you'd do, but what other people do, what they need. You may want to play a game, but someone else might need to do research, and it has to access the library catalog, too."

"Oh." Marcos looked thoughtful. She loved the way Sean did that, made the boy think outside himself. She supposed it was something he'd had to learn, too. And she found herself picturing a young Sean, wearing the same thoughtful expression that Marcos wore now.

A similar expression, Elena noted, to Sean's brother, who had watched this exchange with great interest.

The ring of a cell phone made Sean frown. It was his, so he pulled it out of his pocket, and started to swipe it into silence as he had done twice already today. Something she appreciated, as it signaled he valued their presence more. But this time he stopped before touching the screen. And then, with an apologetic look and a quick, "Sorry," he answered.

His side of the conversation consisted mostly of "Copy," and "Go on." But when he hung up it was with profuse thanks. Then he looked at Slater.

"That was the Inyo County Sheriff's Office, in California."

"Case you're working?" Slater asked with a raised brow.

"Case I've been working my entire career."

Slater went very still. Stared at his younger brother.

Sean swallowed. Then said, the undertone in his voice something she'd never heard from him before, "They found Kane's truck."

Chapter Twenty-Four

"NOT HIM, BUT the truck you and Joey found out about," Sean said, wanting that up front immediately.

"You call your boss, I'll call Sage," Slater said.

Sean nodded. He glanced at Elena, but she merely shook her head as she stood up. "We will leave you to do what you must. This is more important than anything else."

"Mom—"

"Hush, Marcos. Sean must deal with this immediately."

The boy's eyes widened. "Police stuff? Okay."

"Let me walk you out," Sean began, but again she shook her head.

"We are safe enough here, and your urge to do the gentlemanly thing is noted. I know how important this is. Please, let me know?"

He nodded, still feeling a little shaken. She reached up then to touch his face. For a moment he thought she might give him one of those sweet kisses on the cheek, which was so far from what he wanted it only added to his frustration. And then, to his shock, in front of Marcos and Slater, she stretched up and pressed her mouth to his. Hunger exploded in him, and for a moment this was all he could think about, the feel of her, the taste of her, and the simple fact that she had initiated this. He nearly groaned aloud as he felt the swipe of her tongue across his lips, and grabbed her arms to pull her closer. Only the gradually returning awareness of where they were and what had just happened enabled him to finally pull back. For a moment he just stared into those dark eyes, which were now warm with gentleness.

"I will be praying this will bring good news," she said softly.

And then they were gone, this pair that had somehow become the hub of his life.

"Well, well."

Sean was afraid to even look at his brother. "Yeah," he muttered.

"That," Slater said, "has been a very long time coming."

Startled, his head came up. "What?"

"A little credit?" Slater said. "Do you really think nobody noticed the way you've always watched her? From a safe distance, of course."

He didn't even try to deny it. "She scared the hell out of me."

Slater grinned, something he'd been doing for months now, ever since he and Joey Douglas had gotten together. "Not so much anymore, I gather."

Sean was pretty sure his expression had turned silly. And when Slater smiled back at him, it was with total understanding. "James Earl Jones said something like one of the hardest things in life is having words in your heart that you can't say.

You've carried this around for a long time, little brother."

Sean's grin wobbled a little. "I guess I still am scared, because I haven't said it, yet. Got a quote for that?"

Slater thought for a moment, then spoke. "Attribution unknown, but how about 'It hurts to love someone and not be loved in return. But it's more painful to love someone and never find the courage to let that person know how you feel.' I came close to that, Sean. Don't do it."

"I won't." And in that moment he meant it completely. He just wished he had faith that his nerve would hold the next time he was face to face with her.

But she kissed me. In front of my brother and her son. That's like a...declaration, practically. Isn't it?

"Let's get moving, then." Slater's words yanked him back before he spiraled down that particular rabbit hole.

After they'd made their calls, Sage was back at the house in ten minutes, Shane in just over twelve. Sage slipped off her spurs and Shane tossed his gray Resistol hat on the rack, but that was the only acknowledgment to being inside. They gravitated automatically to the kitchen table, where all the family meetings of import had been held since the days of Jess Highwater, back in the fledgling days of Last Stand and when this now sprawling home had been merely two rooms and an outhouse.

"Go," Shane said abruptly, just as he did at the station when an officer had a report to give. And that's how Sean relayed the information, keeping his voice flat and unemotional.

"First off, there was no contact with Kane and it's not

recent." That was the most crucial part, so he got it out first. "But a deputy from the Inyo County Sheriff's Office in California ran a cross-reference of our request for info against tow records."

Several other agencies had done the same, whenever they had time, but nothing had ever turned up. But after Slater and Joey had turned up a clue last June, they had expanded the search and Sean had re-sent the request. Since it was a cold case, most places got to it when they could, although perhaps a little sooner than they would have, given that it was the brother of a police chief they were looking for. Shane would never condone using his position for consideration not granted the average citizen, but if other agencies took his name on the header of the request—and perhaps his Internet fame—into account, he couldn't control that.

"She found a match to the plate, and the VIN. Description matches, down to the camper shell. Towed from a county road about three miles from US 395, north of Bishop. The vehicle itself wasn't running. No personal property left inside. Sold for storage fees after forty-five days."

"When?" Shane asked, his voice tight, his dark blue eyes fastened on, in this case, his detective.

Sean sucked in a breath. "Four years ago."

Shane leaned back in his chair. Sage muffled a sound and Slater let out a low whistle. "That's a six-year leap, Bro."

Sean nodded. Slater and Joey had determined Kane had been in Arizona, working at the Grand Canyon, until two years after their father had died. A decade ago. To now have data on where he'd been just four years ago was just that, a huge leap.

Shane looked at their sister. "Any idea what he might have been after in California?"

"Better climate?" she suggested, shaking her head to indicate she had no real idea.

"Joey might know something." Slater pulled out his phone and hit a speed dial. It was a moment before he said, "Sounds like you're having fun." Sean saw his brother smile, and felt a little tug at the happiness in it. Felt an echo of the heat that had blasted through him when Elena had so unexpectedly kissed him. "I need to know if you remember Kane ever mentioning anything about or in northern California."

Joey and Kane were the same age, and had been lab partners in chemistry class in high school. That had been how she'd come up with the memory that had taken them to the Grand Canyon and the most recent lead they'd had until now.

Sean saw Slater's expression change, then he said. "Thank you. And I'll thank you in person later." Then a wide smile as he said, "I love you, too."

Then he put down the phone and looked around the table. "Yosemite," he said. "She said he talked about Yosemite, that it seemed impossible so much beauty could be in one place."

Sean already had his phone open to his map program. "Less than a hundred miles from Yosemite."

"We should go," Sage said instantly. "Somebody, anyway."

"Agreed. Joey and I never would have found out what we did if we hadn't gone and talked to people in person," Slater said.

"Exactly," Sage said. "Maybe he got a job there, too, like at the Grand Canyon. Somebody might remember him."

"I'll go," Sean said. "I could—"

He stopped when Shane held up a hand. And just now it didn't matter if it was the Last Stand police chief or his big brother reining them in, he ruled at this table.

"I get it, all of you," he said quietly. "And I'm with you. But while this is new and fresh to us, it's still four years old. And it's nearly Christmas. It'll keep another couple of weeks."

Sean saw Slater looking at Shane, wondered if the old brotherly antagonism between the two oldest Highwaters was going to break out anew. It had been virtually nonexistent since Lily and Joey had become part of his brothers' lives, but it could still be there, under the surface. Then, after a moment, Slater nodded. And said quietly, "Two weeks is only a hundredth of the time that's passed since they found the truck. It will keep."

Leave it to Slater to put it in a way no one could deny. Sage looked about to protest, but then her expression smoothed out and she nodded. "You're right. I don't want you to be, but you are."

Sean let out a sigh. "Half the park is probably closed for winter anyway. So anyone who might know something might not be there."

Shane nodded. The sudden burst of urgency receded.

"There's one more thing," Sean said. "We haven't all been together, so I haven't told you yet."

"Is this about her highness, Elena de la Cova?" Sage asked rather edgily.

"Sage," Shane said, his voice sharp. "We owe Mrs. de la Cova a great deal for what she did and tried to do for our father."

Sage's eyes widened. "Oh, my God. I'd forgotten. It was her. The one who tried to save him."

"Yes," Sean said flatly. "If you'd seen her after, blood-soaked and crying because she couldn't save him, you would never have forgotten."

Sage looked appalled. "I am so sorry. That was the stupidest thing I could have said. I won't even try to justify it."

"And that, little sister, pretty much justifies your existence," Slater said with a smile.

Sean silently agreed, although he wasn't quite ready to forgive her so quickly. But when Sage made a mistake she admitted it, and made sure it never happened again. She was like Shane's Lily in that, and Shane had more than once said it was one of the traits that had made him fall in love with her.

"Please, Sean, tell us," Sage said contritely.

He sucked in a breath, and let it out. "It's something she told me. About…that day." They all looked at him silently. "She told me Dad's exact words were 'Not his fault…find him…my kids…tell them.'"

Shane's brow furrowed. "Pretty much what the report

said. He'd never blame George for an accident."

"That's just it. Elena said she assumed then, like we all did, that what he'd meant was that it wasn't George Goetz's fault, and to find us and tell us that. But she and I had been talking about Kane, and she said it suddenly hit her that maybe we were wrong."

Slater and Shane had both gone rigidly still. Sage was staring now. He sucked in another deep breath, then plunged ahead.

"She wondered if maybe what he'd really meant was… 'It wasn't Kane's fault. Tell my kids to find him.'" Simultaneously Shane's jaw tightened, Slater swore under his breath, and Sage's eyes widened. Sean made himself finish. "She said that fit much better with what she knew of him."

They sat there in stunned silence for a long moment. Sean could almost feel his siblings thinking, processing. And then they were nodding as they reached the same conclusion he had; Elena was right, this fit much, much better with who their father had been.

Finally Sage, looking directly at him, said with obviously heartfelt sincerity, "All I've got to say is I'm really glad you guys are adding some very special and smart women to the family."

All of Sean's irritation drained away. Sage might get a little snarly with people, but it was almost always in defense of those she loved. And when she accepted, she accepted completely, as she had with both Lily and Joey.

"A little premature there, Sis," he said. He felt a bit at sea, with no idea if he and Elena could really be headed toward the kind of bliss his brothers had found.

"Don't try and sell that to me," Slater, who rarely drawled, drawled. "I saw that kiss she planted on you before she left." He ignored Sean's flush and added, "Believe me, you could do a lot worse."

"Personally," Shane said quietly, but in that way that hushed them all, "I think no man could do better than Elena." His mouth quirked. "Equal, perhaps, but not better."

And as he sat there at the family table, Sean realized he'd just been gifted with an acceptance he'd never even had to ask for.

Only problem was, now it was up to him to make sure it was necessary.

Chapter Twenty-Five

ELENA MADE NOTE of how willingly Marcos went to bed, and how quickly he went to sleep. Obviously a day spent outside, doing physical things, was the key. He'd begun to protest less once he'd started his lessons with Sean, but this was a new level.

Sean.

She quashed the memory of what she had done, how she had so blatantly—and passionately—kissed him, heedless of who else was present, including her son. She refused to regret it, not when she'd felt him respond in the same way. And after all, he had kissed her in front of half the town.

What was more difficult to deal with was the frustration of feeling in limbo, as if they were suspended somehow, waiting for...something.

She paced her bedroom, wondering how he was, wondering what else they might have learned about the missing Highwater brother. Tried to imagine what it would be like, but the only comparison she could relate to was if Enrique had been missing in action instead of killed and recovered. If she didn't know if he was dead or alive, had no idea where he was, how much worse would it have been? True, if she hadn't known there would always be that slim chance he was alive, but the not knowing would have been horrible. Utterly horrible.

She spun on her heel and started pacing back the other way.

Not his fault...find him...my kids...tell them...

As if she were reliving it, the scene flowed through her mind with the force of the Pedernales at flood. The sensation of trying to staunch blood that would not stop flowing, and of looking into a pair of Highwater blue eyes and seeing the knowledge there, the awareness that he was dying. The words, pushed out against the pain, in desperate need to get them said.

Steven Highwater had entrusted her with those words, and she had relayed them carefully. But she had also assumed, as they all had, that she'd known what he'd meant.

She could remember the hard, unforgiving feel of the curb beneath her as she sat there, her feet in a gutter running water tinged pink with blood, after the fire department had washed away the traces of what had happened. She knew she herself was stained with that same blood—her hands, her blouse, her slacks where she had knelt beside the man she so respected, tears flowing from her eyes. She did not care, and was in no hurry to wash away the last trace of him.

And then she had looked up to see a young man, standing in almost the exact spot, staring down at the wet asphalt as if there were something there that could make it all a lie. It took her a moment to place the third Highwater son, Sean. And in that moment he lifted his head to look at her. She had never forgotten what she'd seen in his face.

Six years later, she had looked in a mirror and seen that same devastation in her own eyes. Devastation, as she realized her life as she'd known it was over, and that it would never, ever be the same.

She fairly leapt for her phone when it chimed a text.

Hope this doesn't wake you. On hold until after Xmas. Then one of us will go.

She started to text back that she was still awake, then stopped. Stared at the unemotional words. Gave a sigh of disgust and tapped the phone icon beside his name.

"Elena? You didn't have to—"

"I can't tell if you are all right if I cannot hear your voice."

There was a moment of silence before he said, very quietly, "I'm fine. Better than fine, actually." She let out a breath of relief. But before she could speak he said, "And all the Highwaters thank you."

Her brow furrowed. "Thank me? For what?"

"For what you did that day. And for what you realized about Dad's last words."

"Oh. You told them?"

"They agree." There was nearly an audible smile in his voice when he added, "I think we're all a little boggled we didn't think of this."

"I think you were perhaps all too close to it."

"Probably. But they thank you anyway." A fractional pause and then, "And so do I. For much more than…this." His voice had taken on that rough undertone that was like a soft brush over her skin.

"No thanks necessary."

Silence spun out for a moment, and when he spoke again it was more briskly. And she wondered if, for him, it was a chance missed…or evaded.

"I know you have your family gathering tomorrow, for the feast day, so I won't expect Marcos. But Friday?"

"He will be there. He is already upset at missing tomorrow." She hesitated, then said it. "You would be welcomed, tomorrow, but as Marcos said, it is a crowd."

"I…thank you. But no." He hesitated, and she hated the way he sounded when he added, "I know, weird."

"You are many things, including that wise and generous, and brilliant and kind and clever, and a long list of things. A list that might include, down toward the bottom, different. But never, ever weird."

"I…thank you."

They were the same words, even with the same pause, but they sounded completely different. Pleased. Maybe even more than pleased. And suddenly she was hungry for time alone with him, time to privately explore what was coming to life between them. She simply did not know how to manage it. Her life was so full of family, with Marcos, and living in her mother's house, and then her huge, crazy extended family. Could Sean deal? Marcos could, but as he'd said, it was because he already knew them all. Even she would be a little nervous, if it were reversed.

"But you will come Saturday? To the house?"

"If you're sure."

"It will make my birthday the kind of special it has not been in a long time."

When the call was over she stood looking at the phone in her hand for a long time. She couldn't quite believe how forward she had become with this man. Quite unlike her strict upbringing, and unlike she'd been even with her husband. She might have declared her independence rather fervently and rather young, but she still carried some aspects of her mother's views on such things. And it had, in the end, brought her Enrique, who as a practiced flirt at first took her as a challenge when she brushed him off, but fell in love with her in the process of trying to storm her walls, as he had put it.

But Sean needed this, she sensed. He would never assume; he had not spent his life collecting adoring females, the opposite in fact. And now that he had grown into the kind of man those females would indeed adore, he still remembered when they would have nothing to do with him. He had changed, had gone from the awkward, geeky kid to the fit, strong, handsome man he was now, but he'd never forgotten.

She doubted anyone ever forgot those kind of scars.

WHOEVER BELIEVED FRIDAY the 13th was unlucky hadn't had his day.

Sean was humming along, already with a successful conviction of a serial burglar from Fredericksburg who'd tried to expand his target area to Last Stand, thanks to evidence he'd come up with when he'd figured out where the guy was fencing the jewelry he stole. He'd even gotten through this morning's testimony well. The all-business, impersonal atmosphere of a courtroom was something he could handle, even if it was crowded. And maybe he could even get through this damn seminar thing. It was, after all, just a bunch of cops. He was used to that. And then there was the possibility of another step in the search for Kane hovering. That was huge.

And above it all was the memory of that kiss. A memory that hadn't dulled at all in the two days since.

There was something about the fact that she had done it, and in front of both Marcos and Slater, that seemed incredibly significant. Significant enough that last night he had almost wished he'd said he'd come to the family gathering when she'd said he'd be welcome. But he'd driven by Valencia's last night, and the feast day celebration had been in full swing, with the restaurant as full as it was on a busy night…just with her family. And that, despite his best efforts, was still daunting to him.

But he would see her tomorrow. In a much smaller setting. Of course it would be with her mother and Marcos present, but he would take what he could get. In fact, the thought had come to him that that might be a good thing, because—

"Sean! How are you?"

He blinked, snapped out of his vaguely forming plan for Elena's birthday and back to the present.

"Lark," he registered. "Hi."

Lark Leclair was a familiar face. Not only had she been in his class at school, and a friend, he'd later encountered her now and then when his job had involved at-risk juveniles. Back then she'd been with Children's Services, dealing with kids who had to be pulled out of dangerous family situations. But she had left the job a couple of years ago, and he surely understood why. Now she worked for a private adoption agency, and seemed much happier.

"Sorry," the petite blonde said with a wide smile, "did I derail you solving the case of the century?"

He didn't take offense at her teasing—it was too obviously good-natured. "No. No, it was...personal."

Instantly her expression changed. "Anything I can do? Can I help?"

Unlike some, he knew Lark meant it. He had once helped find a little girl she'd been trying to save from an abusive mother. The mother had finally snapped. She'd beaten the child and dumped what she thought was the body where it might never have been found, but Sean had pored over everything they had and everything Lark could tell him about the case, and come up with three possibilities of where the mother might rid herself of what she thought of as her burden. The second one had not only been right, but they'd found the child still alive. After that, Lark had thanked him so effusively it had almost been embarrassing, and she'd vowed that if he ever, ever needed anything, she was there for him.

Anything I can do?

It hit him then that quite possibly there was. "I…maybe."

She smiled, and it lit her light green eyes. "Anything. You know that."

He nodded slowly, then said, "I need to get a birthday present for somebody, and I really don't know what."

She smiled at that. "I'd love to help. Can you take a coffee break and we'll talk?"

"I…sure."

They were only two doors away from Char-Pie, so they went in there. Charlie was in the back; they could hear her humming. Her sister, Audrey, was working out front, and the slim redhead greeted them both as she poured the requested coffee.

"She sounds happy," Lark said, nodding toward the back.

Audrey rolled her eyes, but it was with a loving smile. "She's always that way now."

"That happy have a name?" Lark asked. "McBride, for instance?"

Something clicked in his mind and Sean remembered Joey saying something about Charlie and Turner McBride finally getting it together. He found himself watching Lark, admiring her easy way with people, remembering how she had been able to coax even the most terrified child into her arms. She understood people, understood what they were afraid of. Even him.

Give people a chance, Sean. Just one at a time, if necessary.

She'd said that to him the night after they'd given him

an award for saving that kid's life. He'd brushed it off saying it was only his job, ready to run the moment it was over, but she'd urged him to stay, introduced him to people one at a time, and he'd gotten through it. So in a way she'd already thanked him, in a very helpful way. But then, that's who Lark was. Ever willing to help.

"So," she said, "who?"

He'd been only vaguely aware of taking a seat at table she'd selected, in a private corner, but her words brought him back abruptly. Should he tell her who? But then would he have to explain why? Did she even know Elena? Should he—

"Whoa, there, my friend. If I'd realized that was such a complicated question I wouldn't have asked so bluntly."

He let out a breath, exasperated at himself.

"A woman, I'm guessing?" Lark said. He nodded. "That narrows the options," she said briskly, as if they were discussing a dinner menu. Like the multi-page Valencia's menu. And he reeled himself in before he could go down that rabbit hole.

"Business or personal?"

"Personal." He managed to get it out fairly evenly.

"How personal?"

"I..." He had no idea.

Lark studied him for a moment. "Maybe...this is new so I have to be careful but I want it to be more so it has to be special?"

He blinked. "I...exactly. Exactly that."

She smiled, widely this time. "I can't tell you how glad I

am to hear that. You're a great guy, Sean, and it would make me beyond happy to see you happy."

He didn't know what to say to that, so he resorted to a muttered, "Thanks."

"So, shall we work on Christmas, too, while we're at it?" Panic stabbed through him. He hadn't even thought about that yet. "It's only twelve days away, better start now." And then she burst out laughing. "If you could see your face!"

He couldn't help it, he started laughing too. Sometimes, it was all he could do. And as Shane had told him when they were kids, in one of what Sage called his Shane-isms, best to laugh at yourself before anyone else did.

Chapter Twenty-Six

IT HAD ALREADY been a remarkable evening, for Elena anyway. Just watching the way Sean interacted with both her mother, with that almost old-world respect, and Marcos, with that sense of understanding would have been enough, but then she had caught him stealing glances at her, warm glances that reminded her of the fire they struck together when they kissed.

When she found herself wondering if it really counted as having just connected when they'd known each other for over a decade—and when she dithered over what to wear and for the first time in years wished she had something other than black and white—she knew just how deeply she had fallen.

She settled on simplicity, her hair pulled back as usual, a silky white blouse that was piped in black with embroidery in a delicate design on the shawl-style collar, a slim black skirt, and a pair of ankle boots with a higher heel than she normally wore. But that would certainly not be an issue with Sean being a solid six feet tall.

She rolled her eyes at herself; she was thinking of them as a couple, when in fact they'd never really even been on a date. Not like normal people, anyway. They seemed to have been thrown together by chance, then by his willingness to help with Marcos, but he'd never actually asked her out formally. She didn't even know if he wanted to. If she got down to it, Marcos had done most of the asking. Of course it had only been… Her breath caught. Had it really only been two weeks since that day after Thanksgiving?

She took a couple of minutes to settle herself before she went downstairs. Her mother had been in the kitchen most of the day, and since she knew this was one of the ways her mother expressed her love, she had not quibbled.

He was dressed in his customary black as well, although he'd added a string tie tonight, which made her smile. No man wore the monochromatic scheme better than he did, and the black made those ice-blue eyes of his fairly pop. She doubted he realized that. Or would have cared if he did.

She knew her mother already liked Sean, but he charmed her even more with his first bite of the dinner she had prepared. He stopped, his eyes wide, and muttered an awed, "Whoa."

"*Tacos de Suadero*," her mother had said proudly. "Elena's favorite dish, but she refuses to allow it very often because it is cooked in lard."

"As much because it is so much work for you, salting the brisket overnight, then cooking it for hours," Elena said. "That is why we do not serve it at the restaurant."

Sean swallowed, looked down at his plate, then up at her mother. "Is that why you don't even have to chew it? Why it just…melts? And whatever sauce this is, with the…is that chili morita? And then the avocado and cilantro on top… Just wow."

"I do like a man of discerning taste," her mother said.

Sean's gaze shot to Elena, and she felt a little zing.

"What does that mean?" Marcos asked.

"It means," Sean said, never taking his eyes off Elena, "that I know when something's really good."

Elena felt her cheeks heat. But Marcos only nodded and said, "Oh. Yeah, it's good," then dug into his own plateful. He didn't speak again until he out of the blue asked, apparently referring to things he'd heard yesterday, "Why is Friday the thirteenth s'pposed to be unlucky?"

"Many reasons," her mother answered, and proceeded to list all the myths and traditions, including Judas Iscariot, that led to the superstitions.

"Personally," Sean said with a grin at the boy, "I watch out for *Martes Trece*. Seems to me there's a lot more solid history behind Tuesday the thirteenth. Fall of Constantinople and all."

Marcos looked blank, but her mother laughed out loud, and Elena knew if he hadn't won her over before, he certainly would have now with this easy knowledge of both history and what was the "unlucky day" tradition in another culture.

"And here I thought it was simply because Tuesday was named after Mars, the god of war," Elena teased.

"You must bring him here more often, Elena," the fearsome Maria Valencia declared.

She would love to. She would love even better having a more…private place to bring him. She had never felt less than loved and welcome here, but this was still her mother's home.

After the meal Sean began to help clear the table. At least until her mother shooed them out of what she said she was claiming tonight as "her" kitchen, and that the cleanup could wait. It was, after all, Elena's birthday.

When she said that Sean seemed to hesitate, then walked over to where he'd hung up his jacket and took a long, slender, gift-wrapped box out of a pocket. He'd brought her a gift? Elena felt a little speed-up of her pulse, and she wondered if her eyes had lit up like a child's at the prospect of opening a present. He'd already given her so much, but she couldn't deny she was immensely curious.

"I told you this was not necessary," she said as he handed her the small package.

"I know. It's better anyway when it's entirely voluntary, isn't it?"

They gathered in the living room, where Elena had turned on the gas fire, since it was a chilly night and rain was threatening. Her mother brought out glasses of *ponche*, theirs with the *piquete*—a bit of local Outlaw Tequila—the one for Marcos without. Elena sat on the sofa, very aware that Sean had taken a seat next to her. Close, but not too close.

Close, but not close enough.

For a moment she hesitated, looking at the package. It was about the size of a jewelry box that would hold some sort of necklace. She didn't ordinarily wear jewelry other than earrings and sometimes, when she was missing him the most, the charm bracelet that Enrique had built for her, adding a charm that had significance to them each year. There were, sadly, only five of them.

And she realized she hadn't even thought about wearing it lately. She should feel guilty about that, shouldn't she? But she didn't. Not right now. Although deep down, she would have expected Sean to come up with something more unique than jewelry. She hoped he hadn't spent too much.

"Open it, Mom!" Marcos yelped, clearly out of patience.

She carefully undid the bow and the paper. And when she lifted the hinged lid of the box, her breath caught.

Elena stared at the beautiful rose-gold, etched fountain pen she had just unwrapped. She hadn't expected him to arrive with a gift at all, but that it was this amazed her.

"Do you like it?" Marcos asked almost anxiously.

"It's beautiful," she whispered, and thought she heard Sean let out a relieved breath.

"Sean said I helped him decide."

She looked at her son, because she could not quite meet Sean's eyes yet. "Did you?"

He nodded happily. "He asked what you liked. I told him about the bracelet things that Dad used to get you, but he said that was a very special thing and it should stay that way, just between you and Dad."

Her gaze shot to Sean then. He was studying the glass in his hand as if the *ponche con piquete* was actually capable of stinging him. It was as well he was not looking at her, for she could think of nothing to say that would be enough for how that made her feel. That he seemed to want her, yet held such respect for her late husband and their marriage, was a combination she had never expected to encounter.

She looked back at the open box in her hands. "What is the design?" she asked as she lifted out the pen that felt wonderfully balanced in her fingers. The etched design was clearly a tree, and there was a leaf emblazoned on the top end. "Oh, I can see it is a maple by the leaf here."

Sean looked up then. "It's an *Acer grandidentatum*. Bigtooth maple. It grows here, because of the limestone soil. It likes the Edwards Plateau."

Which, she knew, encompassed the Hill Country. "It is truly beautiful. It is a strong tree, yet the design is elegant."

"Like you."

She blinked. "I will take that as the highest of compliments."

"How it was meant," Sean said. He hesitated, then said, "It grows some other places, too. Mostly north of here. Except it does grow in a few places to the south. But no further than Coahuila."

Again her breath caught, and she stared at him. Coahuila, the Mexican state that bordered Texas along the Rio Grande was where her ancestors, criollo people, had come from over two centuries ago. And he'd said it with the slightest bit of emphasis that told her he knew that. And his next words proved it.

"It flourishes in Coahuila, and in Texas. It belongs to both. As do you."

It was, in a very Sean way, the most romantic thing she'd ever heard.

"WE WILL BE fine. Marcos can play his game, and I have reading to do. You children go on. Have a slice of pie for me."

Sean wasn't sure what Mrs. Valencia had said to Marcos, who had clearly had every intention of coming along when Elena suggested they visit Char-Pie to pick up dessert, but he was glad of it. Time alone with her was at a premium, but it was hard to complain when the reason for it was that she was a devoted mother. He had zero experience with that, but he could imagine how different his life would have been if his own mother had given a damn about anything except her next drink.

He'd always vowed if he ever had kids of his own, it would be with a woman who would be a real mother, who wanted and would love her children, not see them as an impediment to her chosen lifestyle.

And the fact that he was thinking about that now, with Elena beside him in the car, barely rattled him anymore.

"Back again?" Audrey Stockton said when she saw Sean. "Can't get enough of that pecan pie, huh?"

He laughed. "Didn't think you'd be here on Saturday night."

"It's been busy. Because Charlie's off with her beau," the redhead said with an exaggerated sigh. "I swear, the two of them are enough to make me swear off sugar."

"Please do not," Elena said. "I cannot imagine these delectable pies without it."

Audrey laughed, and nodded. "It would be worse than making your queso without that secret ingredient."

A few minutes later they were seated at a small table for two near the front window, the only one open. Sean dug into his favored pecan pie, but he watched Elena savoring her lemon meringue. "It is," she said, "the perfect combination of sweet and tart. I don't bake much, so I'm here often."

That surprised him. "Baking is simple. It's just chemistry. Measure the stuff and follow instructions and it mostly works. It's the stuff you're good at—cooking, with a dash of this and let's try this spice that isn't in the recipe because I know it will be good that makes me crazy."

She paused with her fork mid-pie. "I have never thought about it quite like that. But I see your point."

For some reason that was much more gratifying to him than he suspected it should be. But not nearly as gratifying as when she offered him a bite of her lemon meringue, on her own fork. He leaned in to take it, imagining he could taste her as well, and savoring it perhaps a bit too long. But she did the same with his offered bite of pecan, and he had the weirdest feeling something had just been declared between them.

"I have to go to Fort Worth next week." It came out rather abruptly, but he didn't want her to think he'd just gone without telling her.

"Oh?"

"I'm driving up Tuesday night, and I'll head back Friday." Further explanation seemed necessary, so he added, "The PD there wants me to tell them how I found one of their suspects last year." He grimaced. "They're calling it a seminar. Which is silly, since I could tell them in three words over the phone."

Her arched brows rose. "Is that the man who killed those people in the bank robbery, the one who tried to spend the marked bill at the saloon, and you tracked him down?"

He blinked. "I…yes."

She smiled at him. "I do read *The Defender*, you know."

He'd almost forgotten the front-page story in the local town newspaper. As those things did, it made it sound more impressive than it was, at least to him. He'd just been…persistent, and done a lot of legwork until he'd finally found the guy holed up with a buddy in a run-down rental over on the east side.

"I'm just surprised you remembered it."

"I was impressed."

"Slater was the one who caught the marked fifty."

"But you found the man, even after weeks had gone by. What made you stick with it for so long?"

Sean gave a half shrug. "It ticked me off that he thought he could hide out here. That we'd be too stupid to find him."

She smiled at him then. "Serves him right that you caught him here, then." He smiled back. "What would be the three words?"

"I didn't quit."

Her smile widened. "A good philosophy. Did you ever want to?"

"No. I never do, on a case." *It's only personal things that make me want to run and hide. That send me so far down the rabbit hole sometimes I think I'll never find my way back.*

"I admire that," she said, and that simple compliment nailed him to this moment. And then she took his breath away. "I will miss you."

He wondered if there was some graceful, tactful way to say he was so hot for her he could barely stand it. Not likely. Or not likely that he'd find it. "I already miss you." He took a breath. "I'd ask you to come with me, so we could…have some time alone, but…"

"This is work," she said with a shake of her head. "And you deserve every bit of the praise you'll no doubt be basking in."

He nearly rolled his eyes. "I'll feel more like an animal in a zoo, some strange species they aren't familiar with."

She laughed. "That is their loss, if they are too blind to see you have much you could teach them."

Her easy confidence in him made him suddenly feel as if he could sail through this thing, and some of his dread about it faded away. And he suddenly realized that she hadn't said she wouldn't come with him if it had been something else and he'd asked.

"Where will you be staying? I know of a nice place, although it is near the national cemetery."

He went still. "Is that…where he is?"

She nodded. "He grew up in Dallas." He struggled to think of something to say, anything, but could not. "It is all right, Sean," she said softly. "I do not dwell on it any longer, but neither will I pretend it never happened or he never existed."

"I would never expect you to. Or Marcos."

"And that is why I will miss you, Sean. Because of who you are." She smiled at him then, so beautifully it eased his tension.

"I...they're putting me up somewhere."

She nodded, and he watched with some discomfort as she took another slow, savoring bite of her pie. He realized he was staring at her mouth again, and looked away.

Since he'd been so focused on her, he only now realized that the poster on the wall behind her was for the big Christmas Ball next weekend. The fundraiser for the rodeo scholarship program was one of the biggest seasonal events in Last Stand, and usually something he avoided at all costs. He bought tickets, because he believed in the program, but he had never, ever actually gone to the thing. A big room full of mostly strangers in formal clothes was close to his worst nightmare. And so he had no idea what had possessed him when the next words came out of his mouth.

"Are you going to the Christmas Ball?"

And what if she says yes, with a date, you idiot?

"I wasn't. I haven't for years."

"I never have."

She studied him for a moment. "I imagine that kind of thing would not be your idea of fun."

"True. But I believe in the cause. So I was thinking of going this year. If...I could get a date. I mean if you...would you..."

She set down her fork and looked at him steadily. "Are

you asking me to go with you?"

He clamped down on his nerves. "Yes. Would you?"

She gave him a smile then that made every butterfly careening around in his gut vanish. "I would very much like that."

Sean figured he must be grinning like an idiot. And he didn't even care.

Chapter Twenty-Seven

BY THE TIME they'd finished their pie the place was full, with several customers commenting on how the promised rainstorm was arriving. They stepped outside and found it had indeed begun, with big, heavy drops that splattered loudly. Sean felt the usual little jab of anticipation he felt at such times; for all the damage that they occasionally did, he loved the energy and excitement of a good storm. As long as they didn't turn into a tornado-spawning or flood-causing monster.

"Wait here, I'll go get the car," Sean told her; they'd had to park a ways down Hickory Street.

"No, don't." She gave him a smile. "I don't mind getting a little wet. I love storms."

He hadn't expected that. "You do?"

She nodded, still smiling. "Second only to the stars in Texas on a clear night. There's something about them, in the air. The energy, the power if it's a big one."

He heard a distant rumble. "What about that?" he asked.

Her smiled widened. "I have a healthy respect for thunderstorms, but from a safe distance I love watching the lightning show."

For a moment he just stared at her. Then he pulled out his phone and called up his favorite weather app to check the distance and direction of the source of that rumble. Then he looked at her again. "What's your comfort zone?"

Her eyes were actually twinkling now. "Do I detect some of my same enthusiasm?"

"I've loved them since I was a kid. There's a place I go, sometimes. To watch, when it's coming from the north."

"Show me," she said. "Please."

As he drove Sean told himself he wasn't nervous, just excited. "It's a place I found kind of by accident, halfway between here and Whiskey River. It's got a great view that direction, toward the Pedernales. High ground, but you're not on top of a hill inviting lightning to hit."

"It sounds wonderful."

He knew it was going to be a good show the moment he turned off the county road onto the dirt track. They were closer but not too close, and the lightning had already lit the clouds a couple of times. Hopefully when they rounded the shoulder of the hill, where he'd found that small, natural escarpment, they'd have a good view.

That hope was fulfilled the instant he rounded the last curve and a brilliant, sharp streak forked across the sky.

"Oh!" Elena exclaimed.

For a moment he thought she might be frightened, but then he saw her face, and the realization that she was as exhilarated as he was slammed home. He grinned at her, and she grinned back. This was an Elena he never would have guessed at, and for him it was as exciting as the storm.

It was raining steadily, so he maneuvered to back the small SUV into his usual spot. He hit the power hatch button and it started to rise, then he got out and rounded the front of the vehicle.

"We can sit in the back and not get soaked," he said as he opened her door. He knew when she stepped out and instead of running turned her face up to the rain, that she'd meant every word about her love for this. And when his own pulse kicked up he tried to tell himself it was simply sharing this with her, finding something unexpected they had in common.

They sat under the shelter of the raised hatch as nature reminded them who was really in charge. The lightning that was deeper in the towering cloud made it glow ominously from the inside, the streaks that made it outside seeming like escapees from the maelstrom.

And then, in a furious burst of energy three streaks snapped to life, all seeming to charge for the same spot at the same moment, lighting up their patch of sky as if it were daylight. The explosion of sound was fierce, cracking, and they could feel the power of it, smell the distinctive scent of it. It was wild, explosive. Sean let out a whoop in the instant Elena cried out an excited yelp. They turned to look at each other, both of them grinning.

There was a tangible change, the air between them became charged with a very different kind of electricity. And then he was kissing her, hungrily, but more importantly she was kissing him back, as fiercely as the storm thundering around them. Never breaking the kiss, he pulled her down with him to lie in the back of the SUV. At least he started to; after the first second it wasn't clear who was pulling who.

He felt the long, slender length of her pressed against him, and just that was so much better than he'd ever imagined that he suddenly wasn't sure he'd survive this. The taste of her, the feel of her mouth, the dance of their tongues, were fuel to a fire already nearly out of control. And then she was touching him, running her hand over him, tugging at his shirt as if she desperately needed to feel his skin as much as he needed to touch hers, and his head started to spin.

In the back of his mind the warning voice instilled by his father in that long-ago teenage lecture clamored *Make sure, make sure…*

"Elena?" It was all he could manage. But she understood.

"Yes," she answered, and everything he'd ever wanted to hear was in her voice. "Oh, yes, Sean."

As if a lead rope had snapped he was suddenly as out of control as one of Jessie McBride's new mustangs. Had she shown the slightest reluctance he would have somehow found the strength to rein himself in, but now she was sliding her hands beneath the shirt she'd pulled free and the feel of her fingers on his bare skin made him groan.

He clutched at her, wanting her closer, ever closer. His hands slid down her body until he reached bare skin beneath the black skirt he was sure was supposed to be circumspect but had been just slim enough to show him the curve of her delicious backside. His fingers stroked her leg, upward from her knee, trying not to think about where they were headed for fear this would end for him embarrassingly soon. But she was caressing him, stroking him, kissing him all the while, and his desperation was building.

He wasn't sure how he'd managed the buttons of her blouse, and he wasn't so practiced with a woman's bra to do it easily, but he counted it all well worth it when the lacy thing fell away and her full, exquisite breasts rounded against his palms. He caught her nipples with his fingers, and she moaned in a way that only stoked the fire in him higher.

His problem was he wanted it all right now, wanted to be buried inside her and pouring himself into her, but at the same time he wanted to take an agonizingly long time, savoring every lingering moment, and he could not have both. But right now he did what he simply had to do, he bent to flick his tongue over nipples that had already hardened in a way that spoke of her anticipation and sent another jolt of fierce need through him.

And then he felt a tug at his belt, and her fingers brushed over his erection. Even with a layer of denim between them he gasped, and discarded any idea that he might be able to go slow. He muttered what he'd meant to be an apology for that.

"The only thing you need to apologize for is making me wait," Elena murmured against his chest, where she had opened his shirt. "But I think you wearing shirts that snap makes up for it."

She pressed her mouth to him there as she tugged down his zipper, and as she slid her hand in to stroke him purposefully he felt as if a bolt of the lightning still piercing the night had struck him. With his last bit of sanity he reached for the inside pocket of the jacket Elena had pulled off of him and grabbed one of the foil packets Sage had laughingly tucked into it before he'd left the ranch.

Get over the awe, Bro. I saw the way she looked at you when she was here. Looks like you're finally going to get what you've always wanted.

He hadn't believed her. Then.

"Prepared?" Elena said when she saw what he held.

He shook his head, not wanting her to think he'd assumed anything. "My sister. Harassing me."

"Your sister," Elena said, reaching out to take the condom, "is perceptive."

They dealt, a bit clumsily in the back of the vehicle, with the clothing still in the way. She looked at him with such appreciation in her eyes that he almost forgot to breathe. But he was barely breathing anyway, because he knew now that all his years of imagining had fallen far short of the reality; Elena was far more than just beautiful.

She reached out to stroke his erect flesh again, this time rubbing the tip with her thumb. He took her hand and gasped out, "You touch me like that again and this is going to end really fast."

She opened the condom and sheathed him with it, with enough unfamiliarity to soothe his nerves a little; she was no more used to this than he was. Then he was kissing her again, holding her against him, this time skin to skin, kissing every bit of her he could reach. And when she reached down to guide him, when the ease of sliding into her told him she was slick and hot and ready, he nearly lost control right then, and only that this was—impossibly—Elena enabled him to hang on.

The storm had come closer, as if sensing a kinship, but all Sean knew was the feel of her, the tiny moans she gave, the sounds he somewhat distantly realized were coming from him. With each stroke it took more to hold back, and in the instant he heard her cry out and felt her body clench around him, he gave it up and let go. And in that moment he felt all his uncertainties about anything fade into insignificance. Whether he was odd, or different, didn't matter.

If Elena wanted him, he was all right.

Chapter Twenty-Eight

SHE WAS NERVOUS. Elena couldn't remember the last time she'd really been nervous about anything—when you'd been through the worst, what was there left to be afraid of?—but she was nervous about this.

Her first thought was that had Marcos not been babbling about going to "help" Sean at the library since he'd barreled out of bed this morning, she might have hoped he'd forget and she could avoid this. But her second thought had been that her unsettled thoughts about what had happened last night were no match for the desire—no, the need—to see him again.

And although it was probably where she needed to be, she sent Marcos off with her mother to church. Her mother had given her an odd look, not the usual stern glance for skipping mass, but instead a rather assessing stare that had ended with an unexpected smile. As if she was pleased about something.

Or as if she knew.

You don't know the half of it, Mother. You don't know that your daughter, the one you brought up so properly, turned into a mad, wild thing last night.

Wilder than the storm that had sparked the madness. She had become a hungry, voracious thing who found a pleasure she would not have believed possible had she not experienced it. She, Maria Elena Valencia de la Cova, in the back of a car, indulging in beyond-passionate sex. If there was anything more unlikely, more uncharacteristic of her, she could not begin to imagine what it would be.

And she knew no matter what the future brought she would forever carry the image of Sean above her, his body silvered by the flash of lightning, the feel of him driving into her with all the ferocity she had demanded, and the sound of his hoarse, stunned cry of her name.

And his awed, whispered oath as he regained his breath was all the church she needed or wanted this morning. Nor would she ask forgiveness for the most beautiful thing that had happened to her in so very long.

It struck her that perhaps it was not nervousness that was affecting her this morning. Perhaps it was just anticipation, the luscious, eager kind she had thought herself past feeling.

If the worst ever happens, my love, you must move on. I would not want you being alone forever to be my legacy to you.

Enrique's solemn words, spoken she knew because it was the possibility they lived with as long as he wore the uniform, echoed in her mind. But when the possibility had become her reality, she had pushed them aside, certain she would never again love as she once had.

And so when you do, it is with another man who risks his life in a uniform, merely a different one?

She truly did, as she had told Sean, have a weakness for

heroes. And she had finally realized that his reaction to that had been because he simply did not think of himself as a hero.

And then her breath caught, not because she'd heard the sound of the door indicating Marcos and her mother had returned, but because she realized she had just, without hesitation, called what she felt for Sean Highwater love.

She was not by nature a precipitate woman, yet she was calling what she felt for this man after merely two weeks love? Of course she had known him all these years, known of him for longer. And unlike with a stranger, she had no doubts about the kind of man he was; he and his family were too well known to have many secrets hidden away. And if she hadn't been sure, the way he had been with her son would have told her. None of the few men she had ever contemplated seeing had been able to deal with Marcos.

But Sean not only dealt with him, he understood him, and better, actually liked him. And under that generous care her son had blossomed, even in this two weeks gaining a confidence she had feared she would never see in him. And that had changed everything, even her view of the future.

Quite simply, Sean Highwater had changed not only her son's life, but also her own.

"Are you ready, Mom? Sean said he'd be there by noon."

"I will be momentarily," she said, sitting down to pull on her boots.

Then she stood up and took a last look in her mirror. And couldn't help comparing her appearance now, typical, tidy, hair in a neat bun without a strand out of place, to what she'd seen in this same mirror last night, when Sean had reluctantly brought her home. That woman had been someone she'd never seen before, lips full and swollen from his kisses, hair down and wild, tangled by his fingers.

Dear God, no wonder you don't wear it down. You'd cause chaos.

She smiled at the memory of his awestruck words. For a man who claimed to be awkward and ill-equipped for sweet talk, as he called it, he had proven himself wrong last night.

When they arrived, it was Joey who unlocked the door of the library and let them in.

"Elena, hello," she said cheerfully. Then, with a smile at Marcos, she said, "And you must be the assistant Sean's been waiting for."

Marcos grinned, delighted at the appellation. "Yep, that's me!"

"He's in the back, at the end of the hall," Joey said, and the boy took off running. "My, he's changed since I last had him in my reading session."

"Yes. He has. Thanks to Sean."

"Those Highwater men are treasures," Joey said, with the certainty of someone who had intimate knowledge of one particular Highwater man. "But," Joey said with a sideways look at her, "I guess you know that." Startled, Elena could think of nothing to say. And Joey grinned at her. "I recognize the look. From the mirror, mind you."

"It is that obvious?" Elena finally managed.

"Well, not just from you. The way he looked when he said you were coming was what gave it away." She hesitated, then said, "Kind of new, I gather? He looked a little…awestruck."

"I…" This woman had ever been kind, and was quiet in a way Elena recognized, the same way as herself, the quiet exterior masking the fire within. "Last night," she said impulsively. "And he is not the only one awestruck."

Joey grinned. "Good for you both. I'll bet it was a journey, to get to there."

"Isn't it for everyone?" Elena asked, thinking of what she'd heard Joey and Slater had had to get past, his one-time engagement to her sister.

"Yes," Joey agreed, and Elena noticed her touching the crayon-red streak in her hair that betrayed that fire within. "But for you, with your husband being killed in action, and Sean, always feeling the odd one out, it must have been especially…interesting."

Elena studied the woman before her. "I have a feeling I have vastly underestimated your powers of observation and deduction. No wonder you and Slater Highwater are such a perfect match."

Joey's grin returned. But her tone was serious when she said, "I'm just glad. Sean's such a good guy, he deserves to be deliriously happy. So," Joey said, gesturing at the poster on the wall behind her, "are you going to coax him into actually showing up at the ball this year?"

Elena felt her cheeks heat. "Actually, he has already asked me."

Joey's brows rose, and the grin returned. "Damn, girl! Nice work." Elena laughed. She truly did like this woman.

"Next up, Christmas shopping, huh?"

"I have been thinking of that, but first…I think I need a new dress for the ball. Something…different."

"Time for a change?" Joey asked, glancing toward the back where Elena could hear her son chattering excitedly.

"The change has already happened," Elena said, her voice a little tight. "I need to acknowledge it. Salute it. In something other than black."

Joey backed up a step, looked Elena up and down assessingly. Then she nodded, grinning again. "I know the perfect thing. A dress I've drooled over, but I'm not tall enough to carry it off. You are. And you have the manner, that regal sort of look it needs. Shall we go look while the boys are busy?"

And so, on the day after her world had been irrevocably changed Elena found herself, of all things, going shopping.

OF ALL THE things he might have expected, Elena appearing in the computer room to say she and Joey were going shopping was the last.

"Boring," Marcos muttered, and went back to hooking up the keyboards on the three computer stations as Sean had shown him.

He fought the urge to pull her into his arms, because just the sight of her, back to her usual neat, composed self, sent memories crashing through his mind like the thunder had crashed around them last night. Memories of her, naked, wild, that incredible hair sliding over them both as she kissed him everyplace she could reach until he'd thought he would explode from that alone.

He wished they'd gotten stranded out there, trapped by the storm's rain or mud the way some had, so there could have been hours more of that amazing, impossible encounter. If he could have he would have wished the rest of the world away, leaving only them and the storm. Storms, plural, both the one outside and the one they'd created together.

That it had been Elena, with any trace of her regal, elegant self vanished, seared to ash by the inferno between them, was still almost unbelievable to him. If he did not still have the marks of her nails on his back, if he couldn't still feel her mouth on his lips, if he couldn't so vividly remember the taste of her and the feel of her silken bare skin, he would have thought it just another of what he had for years called Elena dreams. The frustrated, foolish imaginings of the boy he'd once been now leavened with the adult knowledge of what happened between a man and a woman.

Well, he'd thought it adult knowledge, but last night had blasted everything he ever thought he'd known about that right out of his head. And he'd been terrified this morning that she would have regrets, that she would wish it hadn't happened.

Then she spoke again, softly, with a husky undertone that sent a fiery shiver racing down his spine. "And thank you again for my most beautiful, wonderful birthday gift."

"I…you're welcome. I tried it, and it writes nice," he said, sounding utterly lame even to himself.

"I was not," Elena said, giving him a look that about put him on his knees, "referring to the pen."

And then she was gone, leaving him trying to explain to a curious Marcos why he was breathing funny.

"I'm lucky," he muttered, "to be breathing at all."

Chapter Twenty-Nine

SEAN RUBBED AT his face and eyes as he shambled down the hall toward the blessed smell of fresh coffee. It had been a sleepless—and aching—night for him, restless, tossing, wishing. And as much as he liked Marcos, he was beginning to see the downside of dating a woman with a kid.

Dating. Elena de la Cova. Him.

Just the thought put what he was sure was a ridiculous smile on his face.

The smile wobbled a bit when he got to the kitchen and saw the group gathered there. For a moment he wondered if he was off by a day; this was a Sunday dinner crowd. Sage, both his brothers, Lily and…Joey. Joey, who had disappeared with Elena yesterday on that mysterious shopping trip.

"So spill, Bro," Sage said the moment she saw him.

"Coffee," he muttered, reaching for a mug. Which his sister promptly snatched out of his hand. He groaned.

"Might as well give it up, Sean," Lily said, grinning. "There's nothing more unstoppable than a determined Highwater."

"Or a nosy reporter?" he suggested with a grimace.

Lily threw up her hands in mock horror. "Don't tag me with that."

Shane only grinned. As he did so often these days. There was so much sunshine and happiness in this house lately it had begun to make him loathe to be around it.

Until now. When he finally, completely understood the feeling.

"Give, Bro," Slater said. "I've never seen a smile like that on your face before."

He glanced at Joey, who smiled at him over the rim of her own coffee. "Don't look at me. I haven't said a word."

He believed her. He knew Joey well enough to know that if she said she hadn't said anything, she hadn't. Not even to Slater, or he'd be coming at him with more ammo. As it was, all he'd said—with a wink—was that he knew how Sean had always seen her, but that the queen and the cop was no crazier than the saloonkeeper and the librarian.

His gaze shot to his oldest brother. But Shane had his best poker face on, although there was a certain glint in his eye. It wasn't the warning kind he sometimes got, when one of the family strayed too far for his liking, but rather a pleased sort of twinkle.

He'd never been so thankful to hear his cell phone, stuffed haphazardly into his jeans pocket, ring. But when he pulled it out and saw the caller ID, he went still.

"Inyo County Sheriff," he said, and the room went still. They all knew.

He answered, and it was the same deputy who had called before. By the time she was done, he was thanking her profusely. She wished them good luck, and the call ended. And Sean stood there staring at the phone's screen for a moment before he looked up. He was aware of them all, but it was Shane he looked at. Shane, who was suddenly more police chief than brother.

"It may not matter," he began, but Shane shook his head. So he sucked in a breath and said it. "Deputy Meadows took a moment to go a little deeper. She looked at the inventory of the truck's contents. And they found a map under the seat."

"A paper map?" Slater frowned.

Sean nodded. His mind wanted to run, to leap down the rabbit hole from the paper map to Kane not having a phone or not one with data access, to maybe being so broke he couldn't afford it, or maybe even to eat, and that could mean he'd end up in trouble, serious trouble, if he wasn't already—

"Rein it in, Sean," Shane said gently. "There's more?"

He gave a sharp shake of his head. "Yes. She said the map was of the west coast. California, Oregon, Washington. And it was folded open, to show from where the truck was northward."

"Any markings on it?" Lily asked.

"No. But there is one more thing." They went silent. "There was a flyer, one of those tourist brochure things. For Seattle."

Sage's eyes widened. "The Space Needle. He always wanted to see that thing."

Slater gave Shane a wry smile. "I guess it's a good thing

you made the command decision to wait on the California jaunt."

It was later, after Shane and Lily had gone, Joey had headed to the library, and Sage sought refuge where she always did, with the horses, that Sean and Slater sat alone at the kitchen table where so many Highwater meetings had taken place.

"I'm really glad Joey figured out we were making it worse for Sage by not talking about him," Sean said.

Slater nodded. "She's amazingly perceptive."

"And yet she's still with you," Sean teased, but Slater only grinned. From long practice he saw something shift in his brother's gaze, and hastened to head off what he knew was coming: questions about his own status. "I better get going to work, or the boss'll beat me there."

"He's going to drop Lily off at her place, so that'll take a good hour or better," Slater said dryly.

"But she only lives over on—" He cut himself off as he realized what Slater had meant, that there would be…time spent at Lily's before Shane actually made it to work.

"And don't think you've escaped," his brother warned. "You've only delayed."

"Yeah, yeah," he said, glad Slater was going to let it drop. But knowing better than to think that would last for long.

In fact, he guessed it would blow up entirely when he and Elena walked into the Christmas Ball on Saturday.

"WHAT'S WRONG?"

Elena was looking at him across the table in the back room at Valencia's. And an exchange he'd had with Joey this morning came back to him in force.

Elena…

Yeah?

Serious?

I…hope so.

Advice? He'd almost laughed then, because her side was starting to sound like the one-word-at-a-time exchanges between her and Slater that had become practically famous even before they'd been a couple. A sign they were meant to be, Sage said.

Please. He'd take all the help he could get, especially female.

I know it's your instinct to keep to yourself, but share with her. Open up. She's the kind who will treasure that, and never abuse your trust.

He couldn't argue with her assessment of him. Growing up feeling different, odd, taught a person early to keep some things guarded, hidden away. He wondered if Slater had told her that, or if she'd seen it herself. Joey was very smart—otherwise she'd never be able to keep up with Slater—so she'd probably figured that out herself.

"If you think it is not my business, simply say so."

Elena's voice yanked him back sharply. Instinctively he reached out across the table and put a hand over hers.

"No, I just was…remembering something." Still he hesitated. This was something he would normally keep to himself, because it was family stuff. But Elena understood worry and loss, better than most. And she'd helped them so much already, by realizing the mistake they had made, interpreting their father's last words. "We got another piece on Kane."

"More than the information you received last week?"

He nodded. "One of the deputies out in California went the extra mile for us, and found another possible clue. He may have been headed north, toward Seattle."

She looked thoughtful. "That would be a very different place from here. It makes sense, for someone wanting…change. Or wanting to forget."

Sean drew back slightly. "I didn't think of it like that, but you're right. Maybe Arizona wasn't different enough."

He sat for a long, silent moment, pondering. He heard Marcos's laughter from the kitchen area, where he was apparently talking with one of his innumerable cousins of various degrees. It made him smile, and when he looked back at Elena she wore an expression he couldn't even begin to interpret. But when she spoke, it was still of his brother.

"It must be horrible, the not knowing. And the missing him."

"And the elephant in the room," he muttered.

"Which is?"

He felt a jab of regret that he'd let that slip. But he had, and this was Elena, and if he couldn't trust her with this then he had no business even sitting here wishing for even more from her. Much more.

"The one thing I know we're all thinking, wondering,

but never, ever talk about. That Kane doesn't look like…any of us."

Elena sat back in her chair, her expression thoughtful. "He did not inherit the Highwater blue eyes."

Sean nodded. "Hazel. Sometimes they looked green, sometimes brown. But definitely never blue. And his hair was lighter than ours." He realized his jaw had clenched, consciously relaxed it.

"So you suspect he may not be your full brother?"

She put it so gently, so simply that he let out a relieved breath as some of the pressure that had been building eased. "None of us have said it, but I know we've all been thinking it. But I did some research, and it's not as simple as they once thought. Eye color isn't just a matter of dominant and recessive genes."

"So…it is possible he is?"

"Technically. Except all Highwaters have had blue eyes as far back as we could find. And her—" he didn't elaborate, as none of them ever did "—family had blue eyes at least back to her great-grandparents."

She studied him for a moment, and he wondered what she was thinking. Second thoughts, on finding out the Highwater history was nowhere near as straightforward as her own?

"I know your memories of her are not…fond. But…could it be you are letting your feelings about her affect your thinking?"

"Maybe." Sean tapped a finger on the handle of his coffee mug. "But if he's…if he had a different father, I always wondered…"

"What?"

He looked across at her. He'd never told anyone, even his family, the thought that had haunted him from the moment he'd been old enough to understand about infidelity and Kane's different looks. But now, looking at her, at those warm, dark eyes, at her encouraging expression, he couldn't hold it back.

"He was next, after me. I always wondered if I was the reason. If I did something, or wasn't what she wanted. If she…strayed because of me."

Elena's brows rose. "Were you not a toddler yourself when he was born?"

"I…yeah. But I was already weird."

He was a little shocked when she looked amused. "Forgive me, *querido*, but I cannot decide if you have an oversized guilty conscience, or an exaggerated sense of your own influence at two years old."

Sean stared at her. His heart was hammering so hard he could hear his pulse in his ears. Not because she had so gently yet thoroughly put his hidden, childish fear in context, making it impossible to cling to, but because of that one single word of endearment. And that there had been no hesitation, no doubt when she'd said it.

"I wish I didn't have to leave tomorrow night." His voice sounded tight even to him.

"And I wish I didn't have to go home tonight."

"The ball," he said, not even sure how to put into words what he wanted to say.

"I will make certain I do not have to go home that night, if you will make certain we have someplace else to go."

His pulse kicked into overdrive. "Guaranteed," he said. His mind followed his pulse, and he was considering and rapidly discarding possibilities—the ranch, no, not ready for that, a motel room in town was too…tacky, it had to be someplace really nice—as he walked back toward his car. And over it all loomed one simple fact.

Leaving her was getting harder and harder.

IF HE HAD had any doubts, the constant ache Sean felt at being even this far away from Elena and home would have vanquished them. Fort Worth was fine, at least it was Texas, but Last Stand had always been home for him. And now it was interwoven with Elena, and the pull was nearly irresistible. The daily texts and nightly phone calls hadn't been enough, although hearing her voice did ease the ache for a while. Until he had to go to bed alone.

But he'd survived. The seminar, which had been both more difficult—who'd have thought they'd want to know every damned step he'd taken and why?—and easier—apparently "I just had a hunch," was an acceptable answer to that—than he'd expected.

And now, as soon as he completed one last task he'd set himself, one that had nothing to do with what had brought him here, he would be on his way home.

His map program called out that this was his turn, and

he slowed. He wasn't even sure why he was doing this, but he felt he had to. Still he hesitated at the entrance. Grimaced at his own indecisiveness, here at the place where so many heroes were buried. Made himself go on, as he imagined many of them had had to do.

It took longer than he'd thought, but mainly because once he'd found the place he was after, he'd spent a lot of time fumbling for the words, words that would never be heard yet he felt had to be said.

And in the quiet peace of this place by a small lake, he said them.

Chapter Thirty

SEAN HAD NEVER seriously dated when he was in high school. He'd gone to exactly one dance, and that only because Lark had asked him to help her show up her ex who had dumped her the night before. He hadn't been sure he was I'll-show-him material, but with Sage and Slater's help, he'd cleaned up nice enough, and Shane had rather sternly pointed out that he was a Highwater, and that was enough for most people in Last Stand. And in his brief stint at college, he'd been too devastated by his father's death to even think about it much.

But he wasn't sure all that explained why he was a wreck now. Why he was sitting here in his car, trying to work up the nerve to go up to the door of Elena's house. Or rather her mother's house, which didn't ease his nerves much. As warmly as she had accepted him, this was different somehow. This wasn't Marcos dragging him along or vice versa, or them being together because of a fluke of timing and opportunity, or an impulse thing, this was…a date.

He hadn't even seen her after he'd gotten home yesterday, he'd been buried in catching up from his three days gone. And she had, almost teasingly, said she wanted to wait until now anyway. Somehow that increased his nervousness. But as edgy as he was, he wanted—no, needed—to see her more. The five days since he'd seen her felt like a year, and he wasn't too proud to admit that.

He got to the front door without breaking into a run. Her mother answered, and after he stepped inside she looked him up and down. She apparently approved of his formal attire, because after a moment she nodded.

"You'll do."

"Thank you."

"I'm glad you took the effort. And I think you will be too, when you see her." Sean swallowed rather tightly, and couldn't think of a thing to say. And then her expression changed, softened, and she added in a voice just as soft, "You have been very good for my daughter, Sean Highwater. I thank you for that."

He blinked. "I…have?"

"I think you will see what I mean shortly. Oh," she added as if she'd only just thought of it, "and I don't want to see either of you until tomorrow."

He had no idea what to say to that. He'd had no idea Elena would have told her mother of their plans. He was grateful when Marcos raced in. At a lifted brow from his grandmother the boy slowed to a walk.

"Wow, you're all dressed up," Marcos said, wrinkling his nose as if he found the idea distasteful.

"Sometimes a man's gotta do what a man's gotta do," he said, giving the boy a wry smile.

"I don't get what that means."

"You will. Some day."

"You and my mom are really going to that fundraiser thing?"

"We are."

"Why?"

Oh, the list I could give you… "It's for a good cause, one I believe in."

"The rodeo thing, right?" Sean nodded. "Did you ever do that stuff?"

"Not officially, no." He grinned at the boy then, feeling a little of his tension ease. "I left that mostly to my brother Shane, because he was the best at it. Well, until my sister came along."

"Do you think I could ever do that?"

Sean looked at the boy consideringly. "Maybe. You learned pretty fast that day at the ranch."

Marcos lit up. "Cool! I'd like to—Uh-oh. I gotta go."

"You do?"

"Yeah. Gran said I had to leave you alone as soon as my mom was ready." The boy's gaze flicked toward the top of the stairs. "But it's Christmas vacation now, and I get to play my game until bedtime!" And then he was scampering back the way he'd come.

Sean turned to look the direction Marcos had. At the vision that had appeared at the top of the stairs. And forgot to breathe.

She wasn't in her usual black, or even black and white. Nor was she in a sedate, businesslike dress.

She was a tall, incredible column of brilliant, pure red, in a sleeveless dress that was cut modestly high at the neck but flowed down her tall, slender body and pooled at her feet, not clinging yet somehow emphasizing every gorgeous feminine curve. And her hair. God, her hair was down, free, in a wild mane of shimmering waves of richest black, flowing halfway down her back. As it had been the night of the storm, by the time they'd finally sated that ferocious need.

Desire, hot, intense, and nearly blinding slammed through him. He reached out almost wildly, for something, anything to remind him which way was up. He found nothing but air, and some part of his brain told him this was how he was going to feel all night, floundering, unable to quite believe that this incredible creature was with him.

She was a living, breathing flame, and she was going to burn him to the ground.

SEAN'S REACTION WAS all she could have wished. It had been so long since she had thought about such things as whether she looked attractive to a man she'd been completely out of the habit. But Joey had been a tremendous help, and had been right, so very right, about this dress. Joey had also told her to forego doing anything with her hair but let it free.

Your hair is what other women dream about and men fantasize about. Unleash it, Elena. Sean won't know what hit him.

What Joey hadn't told her was what the sight of him, in formal wear, was going to do to her. The western-style tuxedo jacket fit him beautifully. And the formal, crisp white shirt with a wing-tip collar, and without the pleated front she found too fussy, suited him, especially since he'd gone Texas with a lovely, heavy bolo tie with a triangular onyx stone.

And the vest he wore underneath the jacket was nearly the exact red of her dress. Had Joey told him? Perhaps not, red was the only color she had seen him wear besides their shared black and white. *I like red…*

As he stared up at her, his dark formal clothes and hair making his ice-blue eyes seem impossible, she found herself nearly shaking inside at the evening to come and the night to follow.

It took all her focus—and a firm grip on the banister—to get down the stairs. She saw him swallow a couple of times, but his eyes never left her. And when she reached the bottom he said, in a thick voice that sent a shiver through her, "You are the most beautiful thing I have ever seen in my life."

"I could say the same," she whispered. "Have I mentioned I not only have a weakness for heroes, but for French cuffs?"

"I'm no—"

She held a finger to his lips before he could deny he was a hero. "Everyone gets to choose for themselves who they think a hero. And I have chosen."

She seemed to have struck him speechless. He said nothing as they drove, but she caught him a couple of times stealing glances at her. And thought herself much luckier to be the passenger and thus able to keep looking at him the entire time.

Jameson House was dressed in its holiday best, inside

and out. The mass of sparkling lights and the silver and gold décor set an elegant tone, and for an instant she felt a qualm. Her dress was so…so…

"What's wrong?"

She didn't think she'd shown it, but then, this would hardly be the first time he'd surprised her. He claimed to be ignorant of people, but if it was true, he certainly made up for it by being perceptive of changes, shifts, like now.

"I'm just feeling a bit…red," she whispered.

He stopped in his tracks just before they stepped into the main ballroom. He turned to face her, reached out and gently grasped her shoulders and turned her to face him. In her heels she was much closer to his eye level, and she met his gaze.

"You are," he said slowly, "incredible. I don't have to see another person here to know you're going to blow them all away. Every man in there's going to wish he was me, and every woman's going to wish she had that dress."

She stared at him. "You know, for a man who insists he doesn't get people, you surely get me."

They stepped inside. She remembered what he'd said about always buying tickets to support the rodeo scholarships, but never using them, and assumed most of the head-turning was merely his unexpected presence. Well, the female heads probably would have turned at the first sight of him anyway.

She felt a flutter in her stomach when she spotted the knot of people to the right: the Highwaters. All dressed to the nines, Shane and Lily, Sage, and Slater with Joey. Joey who spotted her and grinned. She said something to the others, and they all turned. And stared.

"Let's get it over with," Sean muttered.

"You know," she said as they headed that way, "it truly is amazing that those closest to you are all so beautiful."

"That will be true in a second," he said when they were exactly that one second away. And she had the thought she would not trade Sean's way of complimenting for anyone's.

"Holy cow, Elena!" Sage was practically gaping.

"Indeed," agreed Slater.

"You look," Shane Highwater said with an old-school bow, "like the queen my brother has always thought you."

"Or an escaped supermodel," Lily teased. "The red's incredible, and that's some amazing hair, woman."

She stole a glance at Sean, who was studying the toes of his well-shined boots. Joey simply winked at her; she had told Elena every time she wavered that the dress was perfect. *Red has a certain effect on Highwater men, Elena. Trust me.*

"Thank you, all of you," she said simply.

The night became a blur after that. She'd had no idea her presence would cause such a stir, although perhaps she should have expected it given how long it had been since she had participated in any Last Stand social occasion.

They danced, but she was so rusty and Sean so ill at ease she asked if they could stop. He gave her a grateful look.

"Thanks for taking pity on me."

"More on me," she insisted. "It's been far too long for me to dance in public."

"How about in private?" he whispered in her ear.

She nearly shivered at the intensity in his voice. She could not believe it had been only a week since the night of the storm; it felt like an eternity.

She barely hung on through the formalities of the evening, even though they were brief. The band stepped aside as the president of the Daughters of Last Stand came up on the stage to thank them all for coming, and to announce the financial success of the fundraiser; the rodeo scholarship program was now fully funded.

"Won't your family notice?" she asked when, as the band struck up again, he suggested a quick exit by the back door.

"They'll be amazed—and credit you, rightfully—that I've stuck it out this long. I—" He broke off suddenly. "Unless you'd rather stay. This being your first time to this, and all dressed up so beautifully."

She leaned up to put her lips to his ear, and in words that shocked even her, she told him exactly what she'd rather be doing than staying here. She felt him shudder in response. And suddenly he was a man with a mission, to get them out of here as quickly as possible.

She couldn't agree more.

He drove in silence, but intensity fairly radiated from him. She was surprised when he pulled onto the long, winding drive at the sign that read "Hickory Creek Inn." She could see up ahead the large, white building with the expansive front porch, a rounded gazebo on the side facing the creek, and the distinctive lookout tower in the center above the second floor. Tonight the entire building was delineated with Christmas lights and festooned with evergreen garlands tied with wide red ribbon.

She turned her head to look at him. "Here? But they're always booked up far in advance," she said. When he didn't respond she looked back at him, waiting. He shrugged again.

"I called in a favor," he finally said.

"Ranger Buckley?" she asked. She knew the man whose family owned the expansive property, including the inn and its handful of guest cottages was a retired Texas Ranger, so it seemed reasonable they might have crossed paths.

He nodded. "I ran into him over in Whiskey River when I went to pick up Marcos's present."

She knew about the Christmas gift he'd gotten Marcos—a personalized signed first edition of the first Sam Smith book, written by world-famous children's author Declan Bolt, who lived in Whiskey River. She knew Marcos was going to love it, and be even more awed by Sean than he already was. She herself had been moved beyond measure that he'd gone to so much trouble, although he credited Joey, who had met the author at his first ever book signing a while back, with arranging it.

When they arrived at their room and he'd closed the door behind them, she looked around, then turned to stare at him. "That must have been some favor he owed you."

The room was impossibly beautiful. Elegant, beautiful carved wood tables and lush fabrics. Period-appropriate pictures hung on the walls, and the drapes were a patterned red that went well with her dress.

And, of course, the bed. The huge, high bed with a rich, silk coverlet that added a sensuous element to the room.

As if I need anything but Sean for that…

He came up behind her, put his hands on her shoulders, and bent to whisper in her ear. "This is how I've always thought of you. Elegant. Regal. Magnificent."

She shivered at the feel of his breath. "Sean—"

"Let me make love to you that way. Not in the back of a car."

"I happen to have very, very fond memories of the back of your car."

"So do I. I'll never sell the thing. We'll have sex in the back when we're old and gray. But I want this, too."

For a moment she forgot to breathe. *When we're old and gray…* "You mean that?"

He leaned in even closer, and his voice was rough. "All of it."

"Then show me."

He ran his fingers through her hair, sucking in an audible breath as he did. "Beautiful," he said. He lifted the heavy waves to press his lips to the back of her neck, sending fire down her spine.

He slowly, gently turned her around. Then he kissed her lips, and it was the kind of kiss she'd never had before, eager yet slow, knowing yet sparking imagining, thorough yet teasing. He tasted her as if she were the finest of wines, touched her as if she were fragile, and yet somehow he was making her gasp with the power of it.

She was only aware he'd unzipped her dress when she felt his fingers stroking down her back.

"As much as I love you in it," he whispered, and slipped

it off her shoulders. The red fabric pooled at her feet, and she heard him groan. He slid his hands down her sides, then around to cup her breasts in the matching, lacy red bra. And when she looked up and met his gaze, saw the hunger there, heat shot through her, spiraling down to pool low and deep.

She wanted to hurry, but he wouldn't let her. He'd clearly meant what he'd said, and it seemed to her hours before they were at last naked together. And for a moment he just looked at her. Then, in a voice she'd never heard from him before, he said softly, "You humble me."

She could not, simply could not wait any longer. She reached for him, sliding her hands over taut muscles down to lean hips. She moved one hand to stroke his erection. "There is nothing humble about this," she said, and let her fingers curl around him. He groaned low and deep in his throat, and she could almost feel his will break. He moved her hand so he could sweep her up in his arms. He carried her to that huge bed, put her down upon it with a care that made her feel…worshipped.

And she thought, in the moment when he finally moved to fill the hollow ache inside her that, as long as she didn't lose the wild, frenzied lover she'd met the night of the storm, she could learn to love this aching slowness. And when he stroked her so perfectly one last time, she learned the full and total power of this kind of loving as her body sent out wave after wave of sweeping, unbelievable pleasure through her.

Worshipped was definitely the word.

Chapter Thirty-One

SEAN FINALLY, RELUCTANTLY took Elena home Sunday evening—after getting a promise from her that she would join the Highwater clan Christmas Eve. Marcos enthusiastically greeted him—not even asking where they'd been—and having secured his own promise that they would have another lesson tomorrow, he went back to where his grandmother was arranging an odd assortment of things on the kitchen table.

Elena watched him go, then turned back to Sean. "I'm afraid there is something we must discuss…soon."

Uh-oh. "What?"

She nodded toward her son. "Him."

He drew back slightly. Glanced over to where he could see the boy, discussing something intently with his grandmother.

He shifted his gaze back to Elena. "I thought…he was doing well," he said cautiously.

"He is. So much better." He took a relieved breath. "But he is also curious."

"About?"

"You and I."

"Oh. Is that…a problem?"

"I do not want him developing expectations that are…inappropriate."

He frowned. Inappropriate? What was she saying? That they were inappropriate? Or that Marcos might assume…what? What did she not want her son thinking? That they were together? Had she changed her mind about him, about them? Sure, she'd gone to the ball with him, and he'd thought she enjoyed it—and the long, passionate night that followed—but maybe she'd changed her mind. Or maybe he was wrong about how good it had been, or maybe it had only been good for him. Maybe she'd decided he was too weird after all. So was she breaking them up? But was there really a them to break up, officially?

A possibility hit him then, and jounced him right out of that rabbit hole. But he had to be sure, so he said, carefully, "It's not like you to dance around things. What do you mean?"

She drew in an audible breath. "I mean I do not know how to answer the questions he will soon be asking."

"About…us?"

She nodded. "If you wish to continue this—"

"How could you possibly think I don't?" he broke in, nearly gaping at her. "Elena, I—"

She held up a hand. "I understand this. And I feel the same." She held his gaze, and he saw all the heat there he could have wished. "But with Marcos it is different. What happens between us…he will want to know what it means. If you will stay. And I will not have him destroyed all over again by the loss of a man he cares deeply for." She took a visibly deep breath. "Perhaps you could think about what you wish to tell him."

In fact, he had not thought about this aspect. Yet he should have. He'd been older than Marcos, almost an adult, when he'd lost his own father, and it had still been the most devastating event of his life.

He opened his mouth to speak, then shut it again. Some instinct was yelling at him that this was not something he could or should hurry an answer to. It needed to be the right words, said the right way. And for him, that meant wrestling with it for a while.

"I will think about it," he said. "But remember what I said."

"What?"

He reached out and touched her cheek with the back of his fingers. "I don't quit."

MARCOS HAD DONE exceptionally well at his lesson this morning. And since the boy was out of school for the holidays it had been a long one; Sean had wanted to make up for yesterday, when tracking down a lead on a stolen car had eaten up his entire Monday. Of course half the reason it had was that for the first time in his career he was having trouble focusing; memories of the ball and the night that had followed kept distracting him.

Not to mention Elena's rather lengthy kiss of thanks to

him for keeping the boy out of the house on this Christmas Eve morning, so she could finish wrapping his gifts.

He thought a stop for the boy's favorite chocolate cream pie was in order, so they walked over from the department. He had promised to drop the boy off at home himself due to some female gathering his grandmother had planned at the house this afternoon, and that required Elena's presence. Just the thought made him a little twitchy; large groups of women did that to him.

They were early enough that Char-Pie wasn't swamped, and they had some privacy at the table in the corner. And after the boy had paused in his gobbling up of the sweet treat, Sean steeled himself. Elena's words—and her concern for her son—rang in his mind. He thought he'd found the way, but he was having second thoughts about doing this without her. But Shane had agreed, this was a man-to-man kind of thing, and so here they were.

He pulled out his phone, called up the photograph he'd taken last Friday, before he'd started home. He hadn't had this in mind when he'd done it, but it seemed fated now. He held it out to the child.

"You recognize this, buddy?"

Marcos looked, his eyes widening. "Yeah. Mom takes me there on his *cabo de año.*" Sean knew that was an observance of the day someone died, a day of remembrance. Then Marcos smiled. "We go to church and all, and people start out all serious, but when we get back it kind of turns into a party. Mom says my dad would want it that way."

"I'm sure she's right," Sean said, his throat a little tight.

He wondered if his family would adopt that tradition. It might do them all good.

The boy studied picture of the white cross that bore his father's name. "Did you put the flag there?"

Sean nodded. And it took a moment before he could go on. "And he'll always be your dad, you know that, right? And you and your mom will always love him. Just like I still love my dad."

"Sure." Marcos toyed with his fork for a moment. "But…does that mean I can't ever have a dad again?"

And there it was. He hadn't even had to bring it up. "No. No, it doesn't."

"Good." Marcos looked up at him. "'Cuz I was hoping maybe you might wanna…you know."

Sean took a deep breath. "I'd like to try, Marcos. Maybe it won't work, but I really like you, and your mom, and I'd like for us to be together like that."

Marcos gave him a look then, so full of hope and happiness that Sean felt a pulse of something new and almost scary. He'd never really thought of himself as a father figure, not like Shane had had to become, but maybe…maybe… Hell, if it got him a look like that from this kid who'd come so far so fast…

"Do you know why I went there last week, Marcos?" he asked, indicating the picture. The boy shook his head. "To…talk to your dad. To tell him I understood he would always be your father, but that…I really cared about you and hoped it would be okay with him if I tried to do what he couldn't anymore." Marcos stared at him. Sean shrugged. "I know, crazy, but I felt like I had to, you know? He's your dad."

"But he couldn't answer you."

"Not in words, no. But…it felt like he did. It felt like he was…there."

Marcos's eyes widened. "Sometimes, at night, I dream about him. And when I wake up, it feels like he was really there."

"I know that feeling," Sean said. "And yeah, it was kind of like that."

"Then it must be okay with him," Marcos said simply. And gobbled down his last bite of pie.

Sean felt ridiculously light as he walked Marcos to the door of the house. Even the sight of multiple cars parked in the driveway and on the street didn't faze him, not now.

"What is this…gathering?"

"It's the *tamalada*," Marcos said. "I go hide in my room, 'cuz they get really noisy."

Sean grinned. He'd heard of tamale-making parties, but he'd never seen one in person. And just as the front door Marcos was reaching for swung open from the inside, he was saying, "I love tamales."

"Then you must come in and observe the process." Elena's voice sent a shiver down his spine that somehow turned into heat when it hit him low and deep.

And suddenly a gang of noisy, chattering women—he could hear them from the kitchen—didn't seem so intimidating at all, because Elena was there, and he'd walk through fire to be with her.

"Mom, Sean went to talk to Dad."

He hadn't expected the boy to blurt it out like that, and felt himself flush slightly.

"I see," Elena said, looking at Marcos. He hadn't heard the phrase in a while, but instead of irritating him it gave him a qualm. Had he trespassed? Had it been a stupid idea? Was she offended? Maybe he shouldn't have—

"Show her the picture. He left a flag and everything."

She shifted her gaze to him then. And he still couldn't read it. She said nothing, and he realized she was waiting for him to do as Marcos had said. His jaw a little tight he pulled out the phone and showed her the photo.

"Why?" she asked, and now she was looking at him so intently he knew how important his answer would be. And then Marcos answered for him.

"He wanted to talk to him about him and me and you tryin' to be a family, but how he'll always be my dad and Sean knows that."

She looked back at her son. "I see," she said again. And then, without looking at him, said, "Then you must meet the ladies, and Marcos, you must say hello before you retreat. Come along, both of you."

She turned and headed for the kitchen. Sean swallowed, told himself it was because he hadn't expected this, but knew it was just as much because walking behind her, and seeing the way she moved, reminded him of that red dress. Her in that dress was emblazoned in his mind almost as much as her out of it, standing before him like some perfect statue of a goddess. And he'd done his best to show her the proper worship, and—

He yanked his mind off that path before he had to walk into that kitchen and have every woman in there see what he'd been thinking about, because his body was already responding to just the thought. In a flurry he was introduced to cousins, aunts, great-aunts, and nieces. Some part of his mind registered that, as usual, once his last name was given he was neatly slotted into the Last Stand pecking order, and thanks to Shane, his father, and his fathers before, it was fairly high. Nowhere near Elena's, but respectable.

More as a defense than anything, Sean focused on the process, marveling at the efficiency of the assembly line of sorts they'd set up: one woman to remove and dry the corn husks, the next to spread the dough, next the filling, to Elena's mother, who expertly folded the husks—sides to the center, then bottom up, he noted—and then handed them to…Aunt Delores, he thought, to place them in the steamer. He found himself fascinated most with the wrapping process, and the next thing he knew he was not just being shown but had been teased into trying it himself. It took him a couple of tries to get the hang of it, but he gained a nod of approval when he put them in the steamer the right way, on end.

"And that is the sign of a true man," Elena said to Marcos as he watched. The boy had been looking on rather doubtfully as Sean stepped into this process he guessed he had only ever seen women do. "He will take on any necessary task, and tolerate such teasing to do it."

"And with a smile," Elena's mother pronounced with approval that gave him even more hope that they could indeed make this work.

"That chicken in green salsa looks great. Do you ever make sweet tamales?" Sean asked. "I really love those things."

"We shall, just for you then," Elena's mother declared. "Perhaps with some of my homemade strawberry jam."

It was much later, when the tamales were finished and the ladies had departed, each with their family portion of the day's efforts, that he and Elena had a quiet moment while her mother went to check on Marcos.

"Happy *nochebuena*," he said, and she smiled.

"And you, as well."

"Can you still leave? Come to the ranch with me?"

"I would not miss it." And then, suddenly, she was kissing him. Fiercely, with so much feeling behind it that it nearly overwhelmed him.

"Thank you," she said when at last she drew back.

It was a moment before he had enough air to suggest, "I think you have that backwards."

She shook her head. "For how you handled Marcos. Acknowledging his father. For being the kind of man who would think to go to his grave, for the sake of his son."

"I…it felt right."

"Still, it is a very difficult place to visit. As you know, from your own father, and I'm sure that got through to Marcos."

Sean shrugged. Then gave a rueful chuckle. "When I was a kid and we'd go out to the Last Stand cemetery on my grandfather's birthday, I used to picture all the Highwaters there talking, and think about how they'd welcome new arrivals. I figured they'd throw a big party."

She smiled at him. "There are much worse things to imagine. Sometimes I think we focus too much on the death day."

"It's a good way to get through it, and better than moping around all day."

"Why are you speaking of moping on Christmas Eve?" came a cheerful voice from the doorway. Maria Valencia stood there smiling at them.

Sean resisted the urge to let go of Elena and step back. Not even for her mother would he do that. And then he realized Elena was smiling brilliantly at him, as if she'd realized exactly what he was not doing and why.

"I assume I will see you tomorrow, Sean?"

He blinked. "I…yes."

"Good, good. And Elena, you are going with him tonight? Then I shall see you both in the morning." She sounded more than accepting—especially since Elena would be missing the traditional midnight mass tonight—she sounded happy. They must have gaped at her, because she laughed. "Truly, do you think I am blind?"

"No," Elena said, "but I did not expect you to be so…encouraging."

"Why not? If he is anything like his father, he is a good man."

"Thank you," Sean said, although that had clearly been aimed at Elena. "That's always been my goal."

"See?" her mother said. Then, her tone changing to one much more serious, she said softly to her daughter, "Do not do what I did, *mija.* Do not pass up a second chance at love. You will regret it."

Elena went still. "What you did? You…I did not know you even considered another man after Father died."

This time her mother's smile was sad and regretful. Her gaze flicked to Sean, then back to her daughter before she said, very softly, "As I said, his father was a very good man."

Sean heard Elena gasp, and he stared at the older woman as she turned and left them alone. Slowly, they both turned their heads until they were staring at each other.

"My mother…"

"And my father?"

Elena let out a breath. "It makes…sense, I suppose. They had that love of history in common."

"Yes. And a love of Last Stand."

"And," she said, looking at him thoughtfully, "he was still a very handsome man. As you will be."

"And she's a beautiful woman. As you will be."

He was still having trouble wrapping his mind around this; he'd had no more clue than Elena. And then she spoke, in mock horror.

"Dear heaven, we could have been step-siblings."

There was one long, silent moment, until Sean couldn't hold it back any longer and he burst out laughing. And then so did she, and they practically fell into each other's arms.

Chapter Thirty-Two

IT WAS A lovely drive through Last Stand, down Main Street with all the Christmas lights and decorations. But it was a clear night, and once they were out of town the stars seemed almost as glorious to her.

"There is nothing like the Texas stars at night."

"I think someone wrote that song," he said with a grin.

She laughed. "They are big and bright."

"And I'll be kind and not try and sing it."

They grinned at each other, and Elena resisted the urge to at least hum the famous tune under her breath.

"You can still escape, even after tonight you know," Sean said as they neared the ranch.

Elena paused, shifting the pot of sweet tamales she was holding. "I can?"

He nodded. "In the Highwater clan, it's that Sunday dinner that…makes things official."

She arched a brow at him. "So you've said."

"It kind of involves breakfast the next morning, too." He was looking straight ahead, as if the road he drove daily was completely unfamiliar. "They figure if you're serious enough to…spend the night at the ranch, they'd better know you."

"I would hope so."

He finally gave her a sideways glance as he slowed. Ahead she could see the wide gate with the Lone Star in the center, and the Lone Star flag still flew, properly lit of course.

"We've each got a wing of the house to ourselves, and Sage has the upstairs. We usually only collide in the kitchen or great room. Or the media room."

"Is this your way of telling me there is privacy?"

He stopped the vehicle, making no move yet to open the gate. "Yes. As much as you want."

"Something sadly lacking in my mother's house," she said ruefully.

"I wasn't going to say that," he answered, very circumspectly. She waited. He tapped a finger against the steering wheel. She saw him lower his gaze from the gate to the dashboard, as if he'd never seen it before. "Too soon? Or just no?"

She adored this man, truly she did, but sometimes… "What, exactly, are you saying?"

His head snapped around. "I…what do you think…?"

"I don't know. I never heard the actual words."

He went back to studying the dashboard. "Damn, I suck at this."

"I see."

"And I hate that phrase!" Then he sucked in a deep breath and let it out audibly. She saw his shoulders, those broad shoulders that she had admired, caressed, and trailed her mouth over, slump slightly.

"Then I shall try to make sure you never hear it again."

His head snapped around again. For a moment he just stared at her, then, with a look of resignation, he said quietly, "I'll take you home, then."

Only then did she realize how he had taken her answer, that he thought she'd meant he wouldn't hear it because she wouldn't be with him. Logic told her it was the boy he'd once been speaking at the moment, the one who had always thought of her as out of his reach, but that didn't stop it from wrenching at her heart.

"That is not what I meant." She hesitated, then went on. "It is a defense mechanism, you know."

His brow furrowed. "What?"

"That phrase. It is…a habit, when I do not know exactly what to say."

"I can't imagine you not knowing exactly what to say." He grimaced. "I thought…it was you being amused at something stupid, or silly."

Meaning, in this case, him. She drew back slightly. "Truly? That's what you thought?"

He nodded. "Maybe it's just me."

"And how many times in your life, Sean, have you made that assumption?"

"A lot."

"Let's make a bargain. I will break my habit, if you will break yours. I will discard that phrase forever, and you will never again assume you are anything less than the amazing man that you are."

He swallowed visibly. "Wow."

"Deal?"

"Deal."

It was so heartfelt she laughed. "Then tell me, *querido*, are you going to get around to that invitation?"

He turned in the seat and put his hands over hers on the pot of tamales. "I was trying to be careful. Because I never in my life, in all the years I thought you the most beautiful, most elegant, most amazing woman I'd ever seen, thought I would have a chance to ask."

"*Dios mio*," she breathed. This was the man who thought himself strange, out of step with most people? "That is the most beautiful, elegant and amazing thing I've ever heard, Sean Highwater."

He looked relieved. "I know it hasn't been that long, only a month, but—"

"Has it not been years?" she asked quietly.

His mouth quirked. "Yeah. Yeah, it has. Is that a yes?"

"It is indeed. But for now, lead on," she said. "As intimidating as your family is—"

"My family?" he nearly yelped. "How about yours? You have more cousins than I have teeth."

"And to think they could have been combined," she said with a teasing smile, although she was still a little shocked that she hadn't known about her mother and his father.

"It would have been awesome. Terrifying, but awesome." He went quiet for a moment before, his fingers tightening over hers, he said softly, "And maybe, if we don't drive you crazy…if I don't drive you crazy…"

She clasped his hands in return. Because she knew what he was saying. That it might still happen, that combining of families. But she also heard the tension, the nervousness in his voice. "I have a very high tolerance for crazy."

A grin, that brilliant, wonderful Sean grin flashed for a moment. "Obviously," he said.

It turned into a delightful Christmas Eve. Sage was happily buzzing about, organizing food and drink. She took one look at what Elena held and lit up. "If you tell me those are sweet tamales, I will dance at your wedding."

"They are, and I will hold you to that," she answered, quite seriously. Sage's gaze flicked to Sean, who was apparently taking some ribbing from Slater, judging by his expression. But then she looked back at Elena.

"I'm glad," she said simply. And Elena saw all the love this young woman had for her brother in that declaration, before she took the pot and vanished into the kitchen.

Slater greeted her warmly. Joey, whom she hadn't seen since the ball and took aside to thank her for the rousing—and arousing—success of the red dress, then introduced her parents. She recognized them from their regular visits to the restaurant. And then Lily to her mom, a veterinarian who was up from San Antonio for the holiday, accompanied by a man named Travis she gathered was a police captain from San Antonio who was an acquaintance of Shane's.

And then Shane himself, the man she had always admired for the way he had stepped up for his younger siblings. The man who had so much presence he could be beyond intimidating.

"So," he said, holding her gaze with his dark blue eyes, "fate had the next generation in mind."

Her eyes widened as she realized what he meant. "You knew? About my mother and...your father?"

"Suspected," he said. "I saw them together the day I left for college, and they looked..." He couldn't seem to find the word so just went on. "They were arguing about some fine point of history, and I remember thinking there were sparks flying. I didn't realize until much later what kind."

"I always knew how much she liked and respected him, but I never guessed her feelings went beyond that. She still regrets that she hesitated too long," Elena said.

"But you won't, will you?"

"I believe, as they say, Chief Highwater, that ship has already sailed."

Shane burst out laughing, and then gave her a fierce hug that was all she could have wished for from the man who had become the young patriarch of the Highwater clan.

After a much more rollicking Christmas Eve than she was used to, Sean spirited her away via the back door of the house. He led her down a stone walkway, and around a corner to a covered patio and another door, which she guessed led to the separate living area he'd mentioned.

"Dad thought ahead," he said now. "He wanted to be sure we'd all stay."

"He wanted his family under one roof. I can understand that."

He led her into his wing of the house, which turned out to be as large as a good-sized apartment in town. They stepped into an expansive sitting room with comfortable-looking furniture, an entire wall of nearly full bookcases, and a flat screen on the other main wall. There was a separate office with the rather impressive computer set up she'd expected, an alcove with cupboards, a small sink, under-counter refrigerator, a microwave, and a table with a couple of chairs—"Midnight snacks," he told her with a grin—and toward the back a spacious, modern bathroom. All of which were tidy, which did not surprise her. It was also homey, and felt rather welcoming to her.

Or perhaps that was just Sean.

"I stole some cookies, and hot chocolate, earlier," he said, walking over to the table, where there was also a gift-wrapped box. "And I wanted to give you this. And hope you don't..."

His voice faded and he gave a sharp shake of his head. She almost asked, but stopped when he held out the rectangular package. He was clearly nervous, and she found that endearing somehow.

"How odd," she said, and before he could assume that was a criticism she reached into her handbag and drew out her own gift to him. It was almost exactly the same shape and size.

They traded. He was the first to get the wrapping off, and he froze. Stared at the frame in his hands. Her breath caught in her throat. Had she made a mistake? Assumed too much?

But then he smiled, let out a breath and slowly lifted his gaze to her face. He nodded toward the gift she held. She peeled back the cheerful red and green paper and—stared. Just as he had. She knew what he held, a framed print of the photograph her mother had taken of them before they left the night of the Christmas Ball, as they stood neatly rimmed by the arched doorway of the house. It had come out beautifully, but what had touched her the most was how much they looked like...a couple. Together.

What she had not expected was to be holding a variation on the same thing: a framed print of a picture taken at the ball itself. She didn't know by whom, she hadn't noticed. Not because they'd been dancing, but because she was not looking anywhere except at Sean, and he at her, and in that captured instant it was all there, in their expressions, in the way they were holding each other.

Simultaneously they both laughed, and then they were hugging each other.

"I love you, Maria Elena Valencia de la Cova," he said.

"And I you, Sean Austin Highwater," she whispered back.

Then he was kissing her, and she him, and she knew this night would end behind the doorway she had, until now, avoided looking at. The doorway to a separate room she guessed was the bedroom.

His bedroom.

He led her that way, although he looked a little nervous. "Is it so difficult here, in your home?" she asked.

His expression changed to startled. "I...no! It's just...my bedroom's a little different."

"I would expect nothing less from such a delightfully different man." She meant it, although her imagination was racing at what Sean Highwater might consider different.

He seemed to relax a little. "I did it when I was a kid. Dad helped me paint the background, but I did all the rest." She was puzzled now, and stayed silent as he led her to the door. To her surprise, before he opened it, he flipped off the lights in the rest of the wing. "Close your eyes and give it a minute," he said.

Now she was truly mystified, but held her silence. And then, after that minute standing there in the darkness with his hand holding hers, he opened the door and led her in. She opened her eyes. Saw only darkness.

"Up," was all he said.

She looked. And gasped. For above her was a night sky full of stars, her beloved Texas stars. Not random spots of glowing light but familiar, recognizable. Loved.

"Sagittarius!" she exclaimed. "And Pisces, and Capricorn." This, she realized in sudden understanding, was why he had looked at her so intently when they'd spoken of the stars before, when he'd explained about the rabbit holes. "What a wonderful thing, to look up at every night!"

And suddenly she was in his arms, and he was kissing her fiercely. "I knew you'd get it," he said when he pulled away enough to take a breath.

"I love it, Sean. Did you truly do this when you were a boy?"

"When I was fourteen. Took me months."

"Oh, but worth it!"

"I've thought sometimes, when it hurt too much thinking about Dad, about painting over it—"

"Oh, no! You must not. He would not want you to."

"No, he wouldn't," Sean said softly. Then, after a moment there in the dark, he asked quietly, "Do you think he would be happy? About…us?"

"I would like to think so," she said. And then, tightening her arms around him, she whispered, "Will you make love to me here, under our Texas stars?"

In answer he swept her up into his arms and they tumbled to the bed. Elena laughed, feeling lighter, freer than she had in years.

"Merry Christmas," she whispered in his ear.

"*Feliz Navidad*," he answered, and kissed hers.

And it had never felt more right, that they, descended from two who had fought for their lives in this place, and then stayed to build the town that thrived today, found all the Christmas joy she could have ever hoped for in each other.

The End

If you enjoyed this book, please leave a review at your favorite online retailer! Even if it's just a sentence or two it makes all the difference.

Thanks for reading *A Lone Star Christmas* by Justine Davis!

Discover your next romance at TulePublishing.com.

If you enjoyed *A Lone Star Christmas,*
you'll love the other books in....

The Texas Justice series

Book 1: *Lone Star Lawman*

Book 2: *Lone Star Nights*

Book 3: *A Lone Star Christmas*

Book 4: *Coming March 2020!*

Book 5: *Coming June 2020!*

More books by Justine Davis

The Whiskey River series

Book 1: *Whiskey River Rescue*

Book 2: *Whiskey River Runaway*

Book 3: *Whiskey River Rockstar*

If you enjoyed *A Lone Star Christmas*, you'll love these other Last Stand Christmas books!

Christmas Flowers
by Sasha Summers

Christmas for the Deputy
by Nicole Helm

Under the Mistletoe
by Eve Gaddy

About the Author

Author of more than 70 books, (she sold her first ten in less than two years) Justine Davis is a five time winner of the coveted RWA RITA Award, including for being inducted into the RWA Hall of Fame. A fifteen time nominee for RT Book Review awards, she has won four times, received three of their lifetime achievement awards, and had four titles on the magazine's 200 Best of all Time list. Her books have appeared on national best seller lists, including USA Today. She has been featured on CNN, taught at several national and international conferences, and at the UCLA writer's program.

After years of working in law enforcement, and more years doing both, Justine now writes full time. She lives near beautiful Puget Sound in Washington State, peacefully coexisting with deer, bears, a pair of bald eagles, a tailless raccoon, and her beloved '67 Corvette roadster. When she's not writing, taking photographs, or driving said roadster (and yes, it goes very fast) she tends to her knitting. Literally.

Visit Justine at her website JustineDavis.com

Thank you for reading

A Lone Star Christmas

If you enjoyed this book, you can find more from all our great authors at TulePublishing.com, or from your favorite online retailer.

Printed in Great Britain
by Amazon

28395833R00169